Agatha Christie (1890-1976) is known throughout the world as the Queen of Crime. Her books have sold over a billion copies in English with another billion in over 100 foreign languages. She is the most widely published and translated author of all time and in any language; only the Bible and Shakespeare have sold more copies. She is the author of 80 crime novels and short story collections, 19 plays, and six other novels. *The Mousetrap*, her most famous play, was first staged in 1952 in London and is still performed there – it is the longest-running play in history.

Agatha Christie's first novel was published in 1920. It featured Hercule Poirot, the Belgian detective who has become the most popular detective in crime fiction since Sherlock Holmes. Collins has published Agatha Christie since 1926.

This series has been especially created for readers worldwide whose first language is not English. Each story has been shortened, and the vocabulary and grammar simplified to make it accessible to readers with a good intermediate knowledge of the language.

The following features are included after the story:

A **List of characters** to help the reader identify who is who, and how they are connected to each other. **Cultural notes** to explain historical and other references. A **Glossary** of words that some readers may not be familiar with are explained. There is also a **Recording** of the story.

Agatha Christie

They Came to Baghdad

Collins

HarperCollins Publishers
77–85 Fulham Palace Road
London W6 8JB

www.collinselt.com

Collins ® is a registered trademark of HarperCollins Publishers Limited.

This *Collins English Readers* edition published 2012

Reprint 10 9 8 7 6 5 4 3 2 1 0

First published in Great Britain by Collins 1951

AGATHA CHRISTIE™ They Came to Baghdad™ Copyright ©
1951 Agatha Christie Limited. All rights reserved. Copyright © 2012
They Came to Baghdad™ abridged edition Agatha Christie Limited.
All rights reserved.
www.agathachristie.com

ISBN: 978-0-00-745166-1

A catalogue record for this book is available from the British Library.

Cover by crushed.co.uk © HarperCollins/Agatha Christie Ltd 2008

Typeset by Aptara in India.

Printed and bound in Great Britain by Clays Ltd, St Ives plc.

HarperCollins does not warrant that www.collinselt.com or any other
website mentioned in this title will be provided uninterrupted, that
any website will be error free, that defects will be corrected, or that the
website or the server that makes it available are free of viruses or bugs.
For full terms and conditions please refer to the site terms provided on
the website.

Contents

Chapter 1

Rashid Street was sunny and full of dust. It was busy with the sound of car horns and the shouts of men and children selling sweets, oranges, bananas, bath towels, combs and all sorts of things carried on trays. Added to this were the warning cries of men leading donkeys and horses amongst the cars and crowds.

It was eleven in the morning in Baghdad, the great capital city of Iraq.

A short man with a red face and a moustache, looking pleased with himself, turned off Rashid Street. He walked along an alley and into a courtyard. Here he pushed open an office door with a sign: Iraqi Iranian Oil Company.

A young Iraqi clerk left his typewriter and came forward smiling.

'Good morning, Captain Crosbie. What can I do for you?'

'Is Mr Dakin in his room? Good. I'll go through.'

He went up some stairs, along a passage and knocked at the end door.

'Come in.'

The light was on and there was no daylight in the room. Behind a desk was a man with a tired face.

Dakin said, 'Hello, Crosbie. Back from the North?'

Crosbie nodded. He shut the door carefully. It was an old door, but it had one unexpected quality – it was sound-proof. With the closing of the door, both men changed. Captain Crosbie became less pleased with himself; Mr Dakin less tired.

'Any news, sir?' asked Crosbie.

'Yes.' In front of him, Dakin had a paper which he had been decoding. He lit a match, set light to the paper and watched it burn. 'The conference is in Baghdad, the twentieth of next month. Time and place must be kept secret.'

'They've been talking about it in the <u>souk</u> for three days,' said Crosbie.

The tall man smiled his tired smile.

'No secrets in the East, are there?'

'No, sir. If you ask me, there aren't any secrets anywhere. During the war I often noticed that any <u>barber</u> in London knew more than the High Command.'

'It doesn't matter in this case. The conference will soon have to be made public.'

'Do you think it will take place, sir?' asked Crosbie <u>doubtfully</u>. 'Does Stalin really intend to come?'

'I think he does,' said Dakin thoughtfully. 'And if the conference happens, it might save everything. If an understanding could be reached . . .' He stopped.

Crosbie still looked doubtful.

'Forgive me, sir – is any agreement possible?'

'Probably not. If it were only the leaders of Russia and America, I believe the conference would end as usual – in more suspicion and <u>misunderstanding</u>. Bad enough, but no worse than things are now. But there is a third force acting here – that fantastic story of Carmichael's.'

'Surely, sir, it can't be true!'

Dakin was silent. He was remembering a worried face, hearing a quiet voice telling him fantastic and unbelievable stories of huge underground laboratories built in a remote valley far from civilization. Of a group of people who wanted total war – total destruction – and who hoped to build a new world from the ruins of the old.

'Either my most reliable man has gone mad, Crosbie, or else – this thing is true. And if Carmichael is in Baghdad on the twentieth with his <u>proof</u> . . .'

'Proof?' said Crosbie sharply.

Dakin nodded. 'Yes, he's got proof. The coded message came from Salah Hassan, as agreed. Carmichael got what he went to get – he has the proof on <u>microfilm</u>. But they're following him. And they'll have people waiting for him here. They have agents in every country, some in very high positions. There have even been security <u>leaks</u> from our own people – that's our worst danger. How can I be sure that one of our people hasn't already told our enemies about our plans to get Carmichael safely into Baghdad?'

Crosbie looked worried. 'But we go on?'

'Yes.'

'What about Crofton Lee?'

'He's agreed to come.'

'Everyone's coming to Baghdad,' said Crosbie. 'Even Stalin. But if anything should happen to the American President while he's here, we will be in the very worst trouble.'

'Nothing must happen,' said Dakin. 'That's our business. To see that it doesn't.'

When Crosbie had gone, Dakin said quietly, 'They came to Baghdad . . .'

He drew a spider's web. In the middle of the web he wrote a name: Anna Scheele.

And a big question mark.

★ ★ ★

Anna Scheele was a <u>platinum blonde</u>. Her blue eyes looked out from behind strong glasses. Her face had neat, small <u>features</u>; however she had made her way in the world not by <u>charm</u> but by <u>efficiency</u>.

Otto Morganthal, head of Morganthal International Bank, trusted Anna Scheele completely. Her memory, her judgement, her good sense were extremely valuable – that is why he paid her a large salary. He would have been amazed if someone had told him Anna had any interests apart from his bank.

So he was surprised to hear her say, 'I would like three weeks off work, Mr Morganthal.'

He said nervously, 'You're not ill, are you?'

He couldn't imagine Miss Scheele being ill. Even illnesses respected Anna Scheele and kept out of her way.

'Oh no, Mr Morganthal. I want to go to London to see my sister.'

'Your sister? I never knew you had a sister.'

Miss Scheele smiled. 'Oh yes, Mr Morganthal. She is married to an Englishman connected with the British Museum. She is to have a serious operation and she wants me to be with her.'

Chapter 2

Victoria Jones was sitting in FitzJames Gardens, telling herself there really was a wrong moment for everything.

Victoria was generous, kind and brave – and telling lies was irresistible to her. Victoria lied easily and with artistic skill. If Victoria was late (which she often was), the excuse of a delayed bus was not enough. Victoria preferred an exciting robbery in which she had helped the police. To Victoria – with her desire for adventure – a satisfying world was one in which there were tigers and dangerous criminals.

A slim girl with lovely legs, Victoria's features were small and neat. But she could twist them to look like almost anybody.

And that was her present trouble. Employed as a typist, Victoria had been entertaining the other typists with a performance of the boss's foreign wife visiting her husband's office.

'Why you say we can't have that sofa, darling?' Victoria demanded in a high, complaining voice. 'You say there is no money. But then why you take that blonde girl dancing? Ah! You think I not know! And if you take that girl, then I have a sofa and a very nice fur coat —'

When the delighted typists suddenly returned to work, Victoria turned quickly to discover that her boss was standing in the doorway. He had heard everything.

★ ★ ★

So, with only a week's salary in her bag, Victoria was sitting in FitzJames Gardens – and only now noticing the young man at the other end of the seat. He was as good-looking as an angel, fair-haired, with very blue eyes. And those eyes, Victoria thought, were admiring her.

Victoria was not shy about making friends with young men in public. She smiled and the young man smiled back happily.

'Hello. This is a nice place. Do you often come here?'

'Nearly every day.'

'Just my luck that I never came here before.' He sighed. 'My name's Edward, what's yours?'

'Victoria.'

'Why did your parents name you after a railway station?'

'There's Queen Victoria as well,' Miss Jones said.

'Mm, yes. What's your other name?'

'Jones.'

'Victoria Jones,' Edward shook his head. 'They don't go together.'

'You're right,' said Victoria. 'If I were Jenny, it would be nice – Jenny Jones. But Victoria needs something with a bit more style.'

This pleasant moment was interrupted by Edward looking at his watch, and making a horrified noise.

'I must rush back to my boss – er – what about you?'

'I lost my job this morning.'

'Oh, I am sorry,' said Edward.

'Well, don't be. I'll easily get another, and I had fun.'

And delaying Edward's return to work even more, she gave him an energetic repeat of the morning's performance, to Edward's great enjoyment.

'You are marvellous, Victoria. You ought to be an actress.'

Victoria accepted this with a smile and said that Edward had better be going if he didn't want to be dismissed himself.

'And I would not get another job as easily as you. It must be wonderful to be a good typist,' said Edward.

'I'm not a good typist,' Victoria admitted, 'but fortunately even the worst typists can get a job now. What's your job? I suppose you're out of one of the services. RAF?'

'Good guess.'

'Fighter pilot?'

'Right again. They're very good about getting us jobs, but the trouble is that we're not particularly clever. I mean we didn't need to be clever in the RAF. They put me in an office with files and figures and it all seemed <u>pointless</u>. Made me sad.'

Victoria nodded sympathetically.

Edward went on unhappily, 'It was all right during the war – we all knew what we had to do – but not now, in the world of 1950. I'm no good at all. Well – I'd better be going – I say – would you mind if . . . ?'

To Victoria's surprise, Edward produced a small camera. She turned pink.

'I really would like a photo of you. You see, I'm going to Baghdad tomorrow.'

'To Baghdad?' Victoria said, disappointed.

'Yes. I wish I wasn't – now. Earlier I was very pleased – I took the job to get out of this country.'

'What sort of job is it?'

'Poetry, that sort of thing. Dr Rathbone is my boss. He's very interested in culture and he wants everyone to share it. He's opening a bookshop in Baghdad. He gets Shakespeare translated into Arabic, Kurdish and Persian.'

'What do you actually do?' asked Victoria.

'Well, just about everything Dr Rathbone needs doing. Then, in Baghdad, I'm supposed to get everyone joining in – it's a kind of youth movement – all nations united in peace. Actually, it's all rather serious and a bit boring. So, if you wouldn't mind – oh I say, that's wonderful . . .'

The camera clicked twice and Victoria almost purred like a cat with pleasure.

'But it's terrible, having to go now I've met you,' said Edward. 'And the thing is, I've got a feeling there's something not right somewhere.'

'Not right?'

'Yes. I mean Rathbone is very respectable and wise and best friends with all types of important people. But . . . it's just a feeling – well, time will tell. I wish you were coming, too.'

'So do I,' said Victoria.

'What are you going to do?'

'Find another job,' said Victoria miserably. 'Goodbye, Edward, good luck.'

They heard a clock in the distance and Edward said, 'Oh dear – I must fly . . .'

And he was gone, lost among the London crowds.

Victoria, remaining behind, was thinking about Romeo and Juliet. She and Edward, she felt, were like that unhappy couple. Meeting, instant attraction, frustration – two romantic hearts separated forever.

Victoria rose and walked quickly out of FitzJames Gardens. She had come to two decisions: the first was that (like Juliet) she loved this young man and was going to have him. The second was that, as Edward would soon be in Baghdad, she must go there too.

Chapter 3

A small, dark man entered a public telephone box at High Street Kensington Station and made a phone call.

'Valhalla Gramophone Company.'

'Sanders here. Reporting on Anna Scheele. Arrived this morning from New York. Went to flower shop, asked for flowers to be delivered at a private hospital in Portland Place. Ordered coat and skirt at Bolford and Avory's. Neither of these firms known to have any suspicious contacts. Scheele's room at Savoy Hotel was searched. Nothing suspicious found. Scheele took small suitcase and went to sister at 17 Elmsleigh Gardens. Sister is entering hospital in Portland Place this evening for operation. Visit of Anna Scheele seems justified. No sign she knew she was being followed. Understand she is spending tonight at hospital. Has kept her room at the Savoy. Return ticket to New York booked for twenty-third.'

Chapter 4

Somehow or other Victoria intended to get to Baghdad. So first she went into a travel agency. There was no difficulty in travelling to Baghdad. You could go by air, by sea, by train, boat and car — but only if you had between sixty and a hundred pounds.

Victoria had eight pounds.

She asked about an air stewardess job, but found there was a waiting list.

Victoria next visited the employment agency where the manager welcomed her as one of those people who passed through the office regularly.

'Dear me, Miss Jones, out of a job again . . .'

'Is there any chance,' asked Victoria, 'of a job in Baghdad?'

'Baghdad?' said the manager in great surprise.

Victoria saw she might as well have said the South Pole. 'I very much want to get to Baghdad. As a nurse or cook, or looking after children. Any way at all.'

The manager shook her head. 'I can't offer much hope. There was a lady in yesterday with two little girls who was offering a ticket to Australia.'

Victoria didn't want to go to Australia.

'If you hear of anything, I'd even go just for the price of a ticket out — that's all I need.'

Everything now seemed to bring Baghdad to Victoria's attention. The evening paper noted that Dr Pauncefoot Jones, the well-known <u>archaeologist</u>, had started work at an ancient city near Baghdad. *The Thief of Baghdad* was on at the cinema, and a *New History of Baghdad* was in the bookshop window.

Victoria believed that if you wanted to do a thing, there was always some way of doing it. So she wrote a list of possible ways.

Try Foreign Office?

Advertisement?

Iraqi Embassy?

Companies that sell <u>dates</u>?

And transport firms?

British Council?

She added to the list: Somehow get my hands on a hundred pounds?

★ ★ ★

The following morning, Victoria was combing her wild, dark hair when the telephone rang. It was the agency manager, who said excitedly, 'My dear. The most amazing thing.'

'Yes?' cried Victoria.

'A Mrs Hamilton Clipp — travelling to Baghdad in three days — has broken her arm — she needs someone to help her — I rang you at once. I don't know if other agencies . . .'

'I'm on my way,' cried Victoria. 'Where is she?'

'The Savoy. She's an American. Mr and Mrs Hamilton Clipp.'

Victoria hurried out and got on a number 19 bus. On the bus, she noticed a useful item in the newspaper that a woman was reading. She got off at Green Park and entered the Ritz Hotel. Using Ritz notepaper, Victoria wrote herself words of <u>praise</u> from 'Lady Cynthia Bradbury', who had just left England for East Africa: 'excellent at dealing with illness and capable in every way'.

Leaving the Ritz she walked to another big hotel, a favourite of church leaders.

In different handwriting – on the hotel's special notepaper – she wrote words of praise from the 'Bishop of Llangow'.

Now fully prepared, Victoria went on to the Savoy Hotel. Explaining that she had come from the employment agency, she asked for Mrs Hamilton Clipp.

It was Mr Hamilton Clipp, a tall, grey-haired American with a kindly manner, who welcomed her.

'Now, Miss Jones, you'd better come up and see Mrs Clipp. I believe she's with another young lady, but she may have gone by now.'

Victoria panicked. Was she to get so near only to be disappointed at the last moment?

As they walked along the corridor, a young woman came out of a door at the far end. Victoria had a strange sensation that it was herself who was approaching. The young woman passed them and Mr Hamilton Clipp turned round to look at her in surprise.

'Well now,' he said. 'That was Anna Scheele.'

He stopped as he spoke, opened a door and stood aside for Victoria to enter.

Mrs Hamilton Clipp was sitting on a chair near the window. She was a little, bird-like woman, and her broken arm was in a hard covering of white <u>plaster</u>.

Her husband introduced Victoria.

'Oh, it's been most unfortunate, Miss Jones,' cried Mrs Clipp. 'Here we were, enjoying London and all our plans were made – I'm going to visit Sadie, my married daughter in Iraq. Then I fell down some steps in Westminster Abbey. It's not too uncomfortable – but how I'd manage travelling, I don't know. And George here can't get away from his business for another three weeks. Once I'm out there, I don't need a nurse, Sadie

can do all that's needed, so I thought I would see if I could find
someone who would be willing to come along for the price of
a ticket out.'

'I've done a lot of nursing,' said Victoria, offering her
references. 'I was with Lady Cynthia Bradbury. And if you need
any letters writing, I was my uncle's secretary for some months.
My uncle,' said Victoria modestly, 'is the Bishop of Llangow.'

The Hamilton Clipps were, Victoria thought, most impressed.
And so they should be after the trouble she had taken!

'It's wonderful,' said Mrs Hamilton Clipp. 'An answer to our
prayers.'

'Exactly,' thought Victoria.

'You have a job out there? Or are you joining a relative?'
asked Mrs Hamilton Clipp.

Caught unprepared, Victoria thought quickly.

'I'm joining my uncle. Dr Pauncefoot Jones,' she explained.

'Oh! The archaeologist?'

'Yes. I'm very interested in his work, but I have no
qualifications so the Expedition could not pay for my ticket. But
if I can get there on my own, I can join them and make myself
useful.'

'What a nice direct girl,' said Mr Hamilton Clipp. 'We really
are in luck.'

At that, Victoria could not stop her face from blushing red.

Chapter 5

For two days the boat had been moving slowly along the Shatt el Arab. Many times the old Arab man had come down the river like this to Basrah. The other man in the boat was wearing the black and white *keffiyah*, the traditional Arab head dress. Over his long <u>robe</u> he wore an old brown coat with a red scarf. He was a man who looked like thousands of others in this country. There was nothing to show he was an Englishman, and that he carried a secret that could destroy him.

His mind went back over the last weeks: the attack as he came over the mountains; the <u>caravan</u> of camels; four days' walking across the desert with two men carrying their "cinema"; then travelling on with old friends of the Aneizeh tribe. Hiding again and again from the men sent to kill him – 'Henry Carmichael. British Agent. Thirty. Brown hair, dark eyes, five-foot-ten. Speaks many languages. Friend of the tribesmen. Dangerous.'

Carmichael had been born in Kashgar, China, and yes, he had friends in all the wild places of the Middle East. It was only in the cities that his contacts failed him. In every town in Iraq, agents were ready with plans to help him get to Baghdad. But these plans, made months before, had failed. The first had been an aeroplane, but his enemies had found out.

Someone had <u>betrayed</u> him!

So his sense of danger was at its highest as the boat turned into the waterway that ran through Basrah. Hundreds of boats were tied up and other boats were coming in.

The old man said softly, 'May Allah make your path straight, and lengthen the years of your life.'

'*Inshallah*. It is as Allah wishes,' Carmichael said, getting out of the boat.

All around him there was the usual noisy, waterside crowd of people. On the opposite side of the street, passing by the shops and banks, were busy young Iraqi men in European suits. There were Europeans, too. No one was showing any interest in him.

Carmichael walked to the bridge at the top of the canal, crossed it and went into the souk. Here there was noise and movement everywhere. Energetic Arabs marching along between <u>loaded</u> donkeys and shouting children running after the Europeans.

All normal.

And yet Carmichael felt a growing sense of fear. No one was following him. Yet he was certain he was in danger. He turned into a narrow alley, then stepped through a doorway into a courtyard with shops all round it. He went to one where *ferwahs* were hanging – the sheepskin coats of the north. He stood there touching them.

'*Besh hadha*?' he called to the owner.

'Seven dinars.'

'Too much.'

'There are cheaper *ferwahs* in the inner room,' the shopkeeper said.

'A white *ferwah* from the North is what I need.'

'I have one.'

The shopkeeper pointed to a door in the inner wall.

As Carmichael passed across the room, he looked at the owner's face – though he looked very much like him, this was not the right man. He stopped. 'Where is Salah Hassan?'

'He was my brother. He died three days ago. His business is mine now.'

Yes, it was possible that this was the brother also employed by the department. His <u>passwords</u> had been correct. However, it was with great care that Carmichael went into the inner room.

Here were shelves full of goods. And a white *ferwah* lay on a small table.

If they had chosen a gun as the weapon, Carmichael's <u>mission</u> would have failed there and then. But it had been a knife.

On the shelf in front of Carmichael there was a big <u>copper</u> coffee pot. The knife and the man's <u>reflection</u> showed in the shining surface. In another moment that knife would have been <u>stabbed</u> into Carmichael's back.

As quick as a flash, Carmichael turned and knocked the man to the ground. The knife fell. Carmichael ran back into the crowded souk, turning first one way, then another.

Betrayed again!

He was <u>on the run</u> once more. Without money, without help. He came out of the souk at last and walked on until he saw the familiar sign he was looking for: British <u>Consulate</u>. He looked up the street and down. No one seemed to be paying the least attention to him. Nothing, it appeared, would be easier than to walk into the safety of the Consulate.

But he thought of an open <u>mousetrap</u> with a lovely piece of cheese. That, too, was easy for the mouse . . .

Well, the risk had to be taken.

He went through the doorway.

Chapter 6

Richard Baker came ashore from the *Indian Queen* in Basrah, the main port in the south of Iraq. As small cargo boats were often delayed, he had given himself some spare time so he now had two days before he must go on, via Baghdad, to join Dr Pauncefoot Jones.

This was a good opportunity to visit some very interesting ancient ruins across the border in Kuwait. A plane left at ten the next morning – of course, a visa for Kuwait was needed, but it would be pleasant to meet the <u>Consul-General</u> again.

The British Consulate in Basrah had a small gate from its garden to the road beside the Shatt el Arab River, and a business entrance in the main street. Richard went in and was taken to a waiting room off the corridor, which ran straight through to the garden.

There were several people in the waiting room. Richard hardly looked at them, his thoughts happily in the year 1750 BC.

It would be hard to say what made him pay attention to the other human beings. It was, first, a nervousness, a sense of tension which reminded him of the war – of a time when he and two others had <u>parachuted</u> and then waited in the cold of early morning for the moment to act. A time of <u>dread</u> – and it was this same smell that was in the air.

The smell of fear . . .

Someone in this room was in fear of his life . . .

He looked around. An Arab in a <u>ragged</u>, brown coat, his fingers playing with the <u>beads</u> he held. A fat Englishman. A thin, dark-skinned man who was sitting back, his face peaceful. An Iraqi clerk. An elderly Iranian in white robes. They all seemed quite relaxed.

The sound made by the beads had a pattern that seemed strangely familiar. Short – long – long – short – that was Morse code. Richard could read it easily. OWL. ETON. What! Yes, it was being repeated, the sounds made by the ragged Arab. 'Owl. Eton. Owl.'

Owl had been Richard's nickname at Eton.

He looked at the Arab, seeing the traditional black and white *keffiyah* around his head, the striped robe, the old khaki coat, and a ragged, hand-knitted red scarf. There were hundreds of men like him down by the river. The eyes met his but showed no sign of recognition – but the beads continued to click.

'Fakir here. Get ready. Trouble.'

Fakir? Of course! Fakir Carmichael! A boy he'd known at school who had been born out here in – Turkestan, Afghanistan?

Richard took out his pipe, looked into it and then tapped it on an ashtray: 'Message received.'

Fakir Carmichael got up and crossed towards the door. He almost fell as he was passing and caught hold of Richard to steady himself. He apologized and moved on.

After that, things happened very fast. The fat Englishman pulled a gun from his pocket and Richard knocked it out of his hand as it came up. The gun fired and a bullet buried itself in the floor.

Carmichael had passed through the doorway and turned towards the Consul's office, but he stopped suddenly, then quickly ran the other way into the busy street.

The Consulate police officer ran in. Richard was holding the fat man's arm. The Iraqi clerk was dancing excitedly, the dark-skinned, thin man was staring and the elderly Iranian was not interested.

Richard cried, 'What the hell are you doing?'

There was a moment's pause, then the fat man replied, 'Sorry. A silly accident.'

'<u>Nonsense</u>. You were going to shoot that Arab.'

'No, no, not shoot him. Just give him a fright. I recognized him suddenly as a man who had <u>cheated</u> me.'

Richard felt it was best to accept the explanation. After all, what could he prove? And would Carmichael thank him for starting an argument that would bring public attention? If he were on secret business, he would not.

Richard let go of the man's arm.

The officer was still excited. 'It is not allowed,' he was saying, 'to bring guns into the British Consulate. The Consul will be very angry.'

'I am sorry,' said the fat man. 'Little accident – that's all. I'd better get out of here.' He pushed a card suddenly at Richard. 'I'm at the Airport Hotel if there's any problem, but it was an accident. Just a joke.'

Richard watched him walk out, hoping he had done the right thing. But it was difficult to know.

'Mr Clayton is free now,' said the officer.

Richard followed the man along the corridor towards the sunlight. The Consul's room was at the end of the passage. Mr Clayton was sitting behind his desk, a quiet, grey-haired man with a thoughtful face.

'I don't know if you remember me,' said Richard. 'We met in Tehran two years ago.'

'Of course. You were with Dr Pauncefoot Jones. Are you joining him again this year?'

'Yes. I'm on my way there now, but I've got some time to spare, so I wanted to fly down to Kuwait. There's no difficulty, I suppose?'

'Oh, no. I'll telegram Archie Gaunt at the Consulate. You can stay there. And we'd be delighted to have you here tonight. At the moment – let me see – we've got Crosbie of the Oil Company and some young man of Dr Rathbone's who's down here trying to get some cases of books through <u>Customs</u>. Come upstairs and see Rosa.'

He took Richard out into the sunny garden. Some steps led up to the private rooms of the Consulate. Gerald Clayton pushed open the door at the top and showed his guest into a cool hallway.

Clayton called, 'Rosa,' and Mrs Clayton, whom Richard remembered as a cheerful woman, full of energy, came out of an end room.

'You remember Richard Baker, dear? He came to see us with Dr Pauncefoot Jones in Tehran.'

'Of course,' said Mrs Clayton shaking hands. 'We went to the <u>bazaars</u> together and you bought some lovely rugs.'

'The best buys I've ever made,' said Richard. 'All due to your excellent <u>bargaining</u>.'

'Baker wants to fly to Kuwait tomorrow,' said Gerald Clayton. 'I've said that he can stay with us tonight. Now I must get back. There's been some trouble in the office. Somebody fired a gun.'

'One of the local <u>sheikhs</u>, I suppose,' said Mrs Clayton. 'They do so love guns.'

'No,' said Richard. 'It was an Englishman who wanted to shoot an Arab.'

Clayton took a card out of his pocket. 'I have his card. Robert Hall seems to be his name. Achilles Works, Enfield. I don't know what he wanted to see me about. He wasn't drunk, was he?'

'He said it was a joke,' said Richard, 'and that he had fired the gun by accident.'

Clayton raised his eyebrows. 'Salesmen don't usually carry guns. I must get back.' He hurried away.

Mrs Clayton took Richard into the sitting room and gave him a deliciously iced beer. She asked why he was going to Kuwait and he told her.

She asked why he hadn't got married yet and Richard said he didn't think he was the marrying kind. To which Mrs Clayton said, 'Nonsense. Archaeologists make splendid husbands. And are there any young women coming out to the dig this season?'

'One or two,' Richard explained, 'and Mrs Pauncefoot Jones, of course.'

Mrs Clayton asked hopefully if they were nice girls who were coming out, and Richard said he didn't know because he hadn't met them yet. They were very inexperienced.

For some reason this made Mrs Clayton laugh.

★ ★ ★

Richard found his room very comfortable, and his opinion of Mrs Clayton rose still higher.

Feeling in the pocket of his coat, he took out a folded piece of dirty paper. He looked at it with surprise – then he remembered how Carmichael had held on to him when he fell.

He unfolded the paper. A Major John Wilberforce had written that Ahmed Mohammed was a good and willing worker, able to drive a lorry and do minor repairs and completely honest. It was the usual type of chit, or reference, given in the East.

Frowning, Richard thought about the events of the morning: Carmichael had been afraid for his life. He had run into the Consulate to find safety. But instead the enemy had been waiting for him – and willing to risk shooting him in front of other people. It must, therefore, be very urgent. And Carmichael had managed to pass this chit to his old school friend. It must, therefore, be very important – and Carmichael's enemies would look for it.

What then should Richard do with it?

He would keep it until Carmichael came for it – but first he must make it safe.

Tearing half a sheet from an old letter, Baker sat down to write a chit for a lorry driver but using different words – if this message was a code, that would be the end of that. Then he covered the new chit with dust from his shoes and folded and refolded it until it looked old and dirty.

He looked at the original message for some time. Finally, with a smile, he folded it small, then covered it in <u>plasticine</u> taken from his work-bag. Then he took something else from his work-bag, something he had found on a dig. He pressed it firmly into the plasticine. He studied the result with satisfaction – he had just made a beautiful design of the Sun God Shamash.

Finally he put the copy of the new chit he had made in his coat pocket.

Later that evening, when he checked, as he expected, it had gone.

Chapter 7

Travelling by air, Victoria thought, was like being taken on a school trip. Kind but firm air hostesses, like teachers dealing with children, ordered you around at what seemed like every step.

They were now waiting in a large room opening directly on to Heathrow airport. Outside the loud noise of a plane gave the perfect background to Mrs Hamilton Clipp who, Victoria had realised, was a non-stop talker.

'We're all here. Why can't they hurry up? They're running late. What are we waiting for?'

Her question seemed to be answered almost before the words were out of her mouth.

The door from the Customs and Passport Department swung open and a tall man came through in a very dramatic manner. Air officials were all around him and two large sacks were being carried by a BOAC officer.

Mrs Clipp sat up straight.

'He's certainly somebody important,' she remarked.

'And he knows it,' thought Victoria.

The late traveller's appearance was calculated to cause a sensation. He wore a dark-grey travelling <u>cloak</u>. On his head was a very large, wide hat. He had silver-grey, curly hair, worn rather long, and a beautiful, large, silver-grey moustache. Yes, he certainly knew how to be dramatic. Victoria, who disliked theatrical men, looked at him with <u>disapproval</u>.

The air officials were, she saw with displeasure, most <u>attentive</u>.

'Yes, Sir Rupert.' 'Of course, Sir Rupert.' 'The plane is leaving immediately, Sir Rupert.'

'My dear,' said Mrs Clipp excitedly, 'That's Sir Rupert Crofton Lee, the great traveller. You've heard of him, of course.'

Yes, Victoria remembered now. She had seen pictures in the newspapers. Sir Rupert was a great expert on China. He was one of the few people who had been to Tibet and travelled through the unknown parts of Kurdistan. His books had sold well because they had been written with humour and in an exciting style.

Sir Rupert was an excellent advertisement for himself – he said nothing that was not true.

With a swing of his great cloak, Sir Rupert passed through the door to the airport.

'Now then, please,' said the air hostess. 'Take your seats in the plane. This way. As quickly as you can, please.'

Victoria helped Mrs Clipp into her seat and sat next to her. In front of them was the great man.

The doors closed – the plane began to move.

'We're really going,' thought Victoria with delight. 'Oh, isn't it frightening? What if it never gets off the ground? Really, I don't see how it can!'

The engines were making a terrifying noise. Louder and louder, the aeroplane moved faster – faster still – they were rushing along.

'It will never go up,' thought Victoria, 'we'll be killed.'

Faster – more smoothly – no bumps – they were flying – she could see a silly little train below – doll's houses – toy cars on roads. Higher still – and suddenly the earth below was just a flat map.

People undid their safety-belts, opened magazines. Victoria was in a new world. Below her were white clouds. The plane was in the sun.

In front of her, Sir Rupert stood up, carelessly threw his large hat up with the hand luggage and relaxed into his seat.

'What a <u>show-off</u>,' thought Victoria, irritated. She saw with some pleasure that Sir Rupert had a <u>boil</u> starting on the back of his neck – it made the great man seem more human.

★ ★ ★

Stopping first in Cairo en route for Baghdad, Mrs Hamilton Clipp said that she was going to sleep until six, and suggested that Victoria might like to see the Pyramids.

'I've arranged a car for you, Miss Jones.'

Victoria was very <u>grateful</u>, and said so with warmth.

The afternoon at the Pyramids was so enjoyable that Victoria wished she could stay a week in Cairo – perhaps go up the Nile.

'And what would you use for money?' she thought as she sleepily lay down on her bed.

'And what are you going to do once you land in Baghdad with only a few pounds in your pocket?' Victoria decided to ignore that thought too.

Why worry?

Her eyes, tired from the strong sunlight, closed gently.

A knock on the door woke Victoria. She got off the bed and opened it. But the knock had been at the next door, it was another air hostess, dark-haired and formal in her uniform. Sir Rupert Crofton Lee opened the door just as Victoria looked out.

'I'm so sorry, Sir Rupert,' the air hostess was charming, 'but would you mind coming to the BOAC office? Just a detail about the flight to Baghdad tomorrow.'

Victoria went back into her room. Less sleepy now, she looked at her watch. An hour and a half until Mrs Clipp would need her. She decided to go for a walk. Walking, at least, needed no money.

She came out of her room. Three doors down she passed the BOAC office. It had a card hanging on the door. Just as she passed, Sir Rupert came out. Walking fast, he passed her quickly and went on ahead, his cloak swinging.

★ ★ ★

Mrs Clipp was in a difficult mood when Victoria reported for duty.

'I'm worried about the <u>excess baggage</u>, Miss Jones. My ticket to Baghdad is paid for, but it seems the excess baggage was only paid for to Cairo with BOAC. We go on tomorrow by Iraqi Airways. Perhaps you could find out?'

Victoria could not find the BOAC office at first, but finally she found it in a corridor at the other side of the hotel. It was quite a big office. The other office, she supposed, had been a small one, only used during the afternoon.

Mrs Clipp's fears about the excess baggage were justified, which annoyed her very much.

Chapter 8

In an office in London, a man picked up the ringing telephone. He said quietly, 'Valhalla Gramophone Company.'

'Sanders here. We've lost Anna Scheele.'

There was a moment's silence. Then the quiet voice became hard.

'How?'

'She went into that private hospital where her sister was having an operation. That went well and we expected Anna Scheele to return to the Savoy. She didn't. We were sure she hadn't left the hospital. We've just found out. She left in an ambulance, the day after the operation. But I'm sure she didn't know she was being followed. We were very careful . . .'

'Never mind the excuses. Where did the ambulance take her?'

'University College Hospital. A nurse came in with a patient – it must have been Anna Scheele. They've no idea where she went . . .'

'Check all bookings to Baghdad by plane for the next two weeks,' the other interrupted. 'She won't be using her own name. Check all passengers of suitable age.'

'Her baggage is still at the Savoy. Perhaps she'll come back for it.'

'She won't. You may be a fool – she isn't! Check those bookings. She's got to get to Baghdad – and by air is the only way she can do it in time.'

Chapter 9

From Baghdad Airport to the Tio Hotel, Victoria's ears had been attacked non-stop by noise – horribly loud car horns, people shouting, whistles blowing – and the never-ending sound of Mrs Hamilton Clipp talking.

As well as that, there was a thick, brown <u>dust storm</u> in progress. Palm trees, houses, humans were all covered. Victoria was not impressed.

She arrived at the Tio Hotel feeling terrible.

An alley led from Rashid Street towards the Tigris River. At the entrance of the hotel, they were <u>greeted</u> by a fat young man with a very big smile. This was Marcus Tio, the owner of the Tio Hotel.

His words of welcome were interrupted as he shouted orders to servants about their baggage. 'Here you are once more, Mrs Clipp – but what has happened to your poor arm? – You fools, do not carry that case like that! Idiots! – But, my dear, what a day to arrive! And you have brought a young lady with you. – It is nice always to see a new young lady in Baghdad – but, my dear, you must have a drink at once.'

Some time later, her head spinning from a large whisky which Marcus had insisted she drank, Victoria found herself in a white room containing a large bed, a dressing-table, a wardrobe and two comfortable chairs.

The dust had changed Victoria's hair from black to red-brown and her face was sore. She pulled aside the curtain and looked out onto a wide balcony above the river. But there was nothing to be seen of the Tigris, only thick dust.

★ ★ ★

After a bath, lunch and a long sleep, Victoria stepped out on to the balcony and looked with approval across the Tigris. The dust storm had passed and she could see palm trees and houses in the pale light.

Voices came up from the garden below. Mrs Hamilton Clipp was talking with one of those sun-tanned Englishwomen who can always be found in any foreign city.

'. . . and I really don't know what I'd have done without her,' Mrs Clipp was saying. 'She's the sweetest girl you can imagine. And very well connected. A niece of the Bishop of Llangow.'

'Bishop of Llangow? Nonsense, there's no such person,' said the other woman.

Victoria frowned. She recognized the type of Englishwoman who is unlikely to be <u>tricked</u> by false bishops.

'Perhaps I got the name wrong,' Mrs Clipp said doubtfully. 'But she certainly is a very charming and capable girl.'

'Ha!' the voice said.

Victoria decided to avoid this lady and started to consider her situation. She was sure the Tio Hotel was expensive – and Mrs Clipp would not be paying for her. Travelling expenses to Baghdad were what Mrs Clipp had offered. The contract was completed. Mrs Hamilton Clipp would leave on the evening train to Kirkuk – and that was the end of that.

What then must Victoria do? The answer came immediately. Find Edward, of course, and Edward must find her a job.

With some <u>irritation</u>, she realized that she did not know Edward's last name. But he had come to Baghdad as the secretary of a Dr Rathbone – an important man.

Victoria went downstairs in search of information. Going through the hall, she went out on to the terrace by the river. Somebody spoke from behind her.

'I must introduce myself. I'm Mrs Cardew Trench. I believe you arrived with Mrs Hamilton Clipp.'

It was the Englishwoman. She had the loud voice of someone used to giving orders. She was drinking whisky.

'Yes,' said Victoria, wishing to escape quickly. 'I did.'

'She told me you were the niece of the Bishop of Llangow.'

Victoria collected her strength. 'Did she really?' she asked with a polite smile.

'Got it wrong, I suppose?'

Victoria smiled. 'Americans do get some of our names wrong. It does sound like Llangow. My uncle is the Bishop of Languao?'

'Languao?'

'Yes – in the Pacific. He's a Colonial Bishop, of course.'

'Oh, a Colonial Bishop,' said Mrs Cardew Trench. 'That explains it.'

Victoria thought with pride that it explained it very well!

'And what are you doing here?' continued Mrs Cardew Trench.

Looking for a young man I talked to for a few moments in a public square in London was not really an answer that Victoria could give. Remembering what she had told Mrs Clipp, she said, 'I'm joining my uncle, Dr Pauncefoot Jones.'

'Oh, so that's who you are.' Mrs Cardew Trench was delighted at having found out who Victoria was connected to. 'He's a charming little man, though he's always forgetting things. I heard him talk last year in London – excellent speaker – I couldn't understand a word, though. Yes, he passed through Baghdad about two weeks ago. I think he mentioned some girls were coming out later on.'

Now it was clear that she was respectable, Victoria asked, 'Do you know if Dr Rathbone is here?'

'He just arrived,' said Mrs Cardew Trench. '"World Brotherhood". What nonsense! All this poetry and translating

Shakespeare and Wordsworth into Arabic. "A primrose by the river's <u>brim</u>." What's the good of that to people who have never seen such a flower?'

'Where is he staying, do you know?'

'At the Babylonian Palace Hotel, I believe. But his offices are up near the Museum. The <u>Olive Branch</u> – silly name. Full of young women in trousers,' she said, clearly shocked at such a modern style of dress.

'I know his secretary slightly,' said Victoria.

'Oh yes, that young man Edward – nice boy – too good for that long-haired crowd of people – he did well in the war, I hear. Still a job's a job, I suppose. Good-looking boy – those serious young women are interested in him, I imagine.'

Victoria began to feel rather <u>jealous</u>.

'The Olive Branch,' she said. 'Where did you say it was?'

'Up past the second bridge. Off Rashid Street – not far from the Copper Bazaar. And how's Mrs Pauncefoot Jones?' continued Mrs Cardew Trench. 'Coming soon? I hear she's been in poor health?'

But Victoria had what she wanted and was taking no more risks. She looked at her wrist-watch and cried, 'Oh dear – I promised to wake Mrs Clipp and help her prepare for the journey. I must fly.'

Chapter 10

Victoria woke to a morning of bright sunshine and went out on to the balcony. Sitting a little way along was a man with grey hair curling down on to his red-brown neck. With surprise, Victoria recognized Sir Rupert Crofton Lee.

Why she was surprised, she could not say. Perhaps because she thought an important man such as Sir Rupert would have been staying at the Embassy. But here he was, staring at the Tigris.

After breakfast, Victoria went to look for the Olive Branch.

Baghdad was completely different from her idea of it – people shouting and a main road filled with cars, sounding their horns angrily. In the shop windows there was a strange mixture of European goods: babies' shoes and woollen clothes, toothpaste and face creams, electric torches and china cups and saucers, all shown together. Most people wore poor quality Western clothes, bits of old army uniforms; and there were a few figures with long black clothes, their faces covered, who went almost unnoticed. Women with dirty babies in their arms asking for money came up to her. The road was in poor condition with the occasional large hole.

She felt lost and far from home. Here there was no beauty, only confusion. She came to the first bridge, passed it and went on. And slowly a kind of delight came over her — the pleasure of seeing all sorts of goods coming from all over the world to satisfy the desires of so many different people.

And then she heard a great <u>hammering</u> on metal. Looking along an alley, Victoria saw the Copper Bazaar. For the next hour she forgot the Olive Branch. The Copper Bazaar delighted her. The <u>blow-lamps</u>, the red-hot metal, the whole process of making things with copper was wonderful. She walked slowly through the souk, came out of the Copper Bazaar and saw bright striped horse blankets, cotton bedcovers, and huge rolls of cheap cottons in pretty colours.

Occasionally, with its owner shouting 'Balek, Balek,' a loaded donkey pushed past her, or men carrying heavy loads on their backs. Little boys carrying trays round their necks pushed their goods towards her with loud calls to buy. Victoria walked in a happy dream. At every turn under the large cool arches and in the alleys, you came to something unexpected – men sitting sewing, a line of watches and cheap jewellery, expensive and richly coloured cloth.

'Balek! '

A donkey carrying a huge load made Victoria step aside into a dark alley that turned and twisted between tall houses. There, by chance, she looked into a courtyard and at its far side was a doorway with a huge sign: THE OLIVE BRANCH.

Happily, Victoria ran across the courtyard and through the open door. She found herself in a poorly-lit room with tables covered with books and magazines and more books on shelves and groups of chairs here and there.

Out of the darkness a young woman said in careful English, 'Can I help you?'

She wore trousers and an orange shirt and had dull black hair. She had large, sad, dark eyes and a heavy nose.

'Is – is Dr Rathbone here?' Victoria asked.

It was maddening not to know Edward's last name!

'Yes. Dr Rathbone. The Olive Branch. You wish to join us? Yes? That will be very nice.'

'Well, perhaps. Can I see Dr Rathbone, please?'

The young woman smiled in a tired way. 'We do not interrupt. I have a form. I tell you all about everything. Then you write your name. It is two dinars, please.'

'I'm not sure yet that I want to join,' said Victoria, worried about the money. 'I'd like to see Dr Rathbone – or his secretary. His secretary would be fine.'

'I explain to you everything. We all are friends here, friends together, friends for the future – reading very fine educational books – speaking poems to each other.'

'Dr Rathbone's secretary,' said Victoria loudly and clearly. 'He particularly told me to ask for him.'

A growing <u>determination</u> to win the argument showed on the young woman's face.

'Not today,' she said. 'We do not interrupt.'

Unhappily, instead of the Olive Branch creating friendly feelings, it seemed to be having the opposite effect.

'I have just arrived from England,' Victoria insisted. 'Please take me to Dr Rathbone at once! At once!'

The young woman turned and led Victoria to the back of the room, up a staircase and along a passage. She knocked at a door.

'Come in.'

Victoria's guide opened the door. 'It is a lady from England for you.'

From behind a large desk covered with papers, an important-looking, white-haired man of about sixty got up. He looked kind and charming and welcomed Victoria with a warm smile. They shook hands.

'So you've just come out from England,' he said.

'Yes. I'm a friend of Edward's.'

'Why, what a lovely surprise for him when he gets back,' said Dr Rathbone.

'Back?' said Victoria.

'Yes, Edward's at Basrah. I had to send him down there to see about some books. There have been the most annoying problems with Customs. Edward's good at that sort of thing. He's a fine young man.'

His eyes twinkled. 'But I don't suppose I need to sing Edward's praises to you, young lady?'

'When — when will Edward be back from Basrah?' asked Victoria hopefully.

'Not till he's finished the job — and you can't hurry things in this country. Tell me where you are staying and I'll make sure he gets in touch as soon as he's here.'

'I was wondering if I could do some work here?' Victoria spoke urgently, thinking of her money troubles.

'Yes, of course, you can be most valuable,' said Dr Rathbone warmly. 'Our work is going very well — but there's lots more to do. I've got thirty volunteers already — all of them very enthusiastic!'

Volunteering would not help Victoria.

'I really wanted a paid job,' she said.

'Oh dear!' Dr Rathbone lost his smile. 'That's difficult. Our paid staff is very small — and with the volunteers, it's enough.'

'I really must find a job,' explained Victoria.

'My dear young lady, I hope you'll help us in your spare time. Most of our workers have their own jobs. You'll find it a great experience to help us. There must be an end to all the violence in the world, the wars, the misunderstandings. A common meeting ground, that's what we need. Drama, art, poetry — the great things of the heart — no room there for jealousy or hatred.'

'N-no,' said Victoria doubtfully.

'I've had *A Midsummer Night's Dream* translated into forty languages,' said Dr Rathbone. 'Forty different groups of young people all reading the same wonderful literature. Young people — that's the secret. It's the young who must get together. For example that girl, Catherine, who brought you up here. She's a Syrian from Damascus. Normally, you and she would never have met. But at the Olive Branch you and she and many others all meet and like each other – that's how the world is <u>meant to be</u>.'

Victoria could not help thinking that Dr Rathbone was fooling himself. She and Catherine, for instance, had not liked each other at all. And Victoria strongly suspected that the more they saw of each other, the greater their dislike would grow.

'Edward's excellent,' said Dr Rathbone. 'Friends with everybody. All the girls admire Edward, they'll do anything for him. He and Catherine get on particularly well.'

'Indeed,' said Victoria coldly. Her dislike of Catherine grew even stronger.

'Well,' said Dr Rathbone smiling, 'come and help us if you can.' He shook her hand warmly.

Downstairs, Catherine was talking to a girl who had just come in with a suitcase. She was a good–looking, dark–haired girl, and Victoria thought she had seen her before. But the girl looked at her without any recognition.

Forcing herself to say goodbye politely to Catherine, Victoria went out.

She returned to the hotel. Trying not to think about her own problems – a girl in Baghdad without any money – instead she considered Dr Rathbone and the Olive Branch. Edward had an idea that there was something 'not right' about Dr Rathbone. But Victoria thought that he was just one of those people who are so sure of what they believe, that they cannot see what the world is really like.

Chapter 11

Victoria arrived back at the Hotel Tio with sore feet. Marcus, who was sitting out on the terrace overlooking the river and talking to a thin, rather tired-looking, middle-aged man, called out to her enthusiastically.

'Come and have a drink with us, Miss Jones. This is Mr Dakin. Now then, my dear, what will you have?'

Victoria said she would have a cocktail and, she suggested hopefully, some of those lovely nuts.

Mr Dakin said in a sad voice that he would have a lemonade and Marcus gave the order in rapid Arabic.

'Ah,' cried Marcus, 'here is Mrs Cardew Trench. You know Mr Dakin? What will you have?'

'Gin and lime,' said Mrs Cardew Trench, nodding to Dakin. 'You look hot,' she added to Victoria.

'I've been walking around, seeing the city.'

When the drinks came, Victoria ate a large plateful of nuts and some potato chips.

After a while, a short, solid-looking man came up the steps and Marcus introduced him to Victoria as Captain Crosbie.

'Just arrived?' he asked her.

'Yesterday.'

'I didn't think I had seen you before.'

'She is very nice and beautiful, is she not?' said Marcus joyfully. 'Oh yes, it is very nice to have Miss Victoria. I will give a very nice party for her. Oh, it is very good. We will have a long dinner that goes on for hours.'

'That will be lovely,' said Victoria, feeling quite weak with hunger.

'I thought you'd gone to Basrah,' said Mrs Cardew Trench to Crosbie.

'I got back yesterday,' said Crosbie.

He looked up at the balcony.

'Who's that?' he asked. 'The man in the big hat.'

'That, my dear, is Sir Rupert Crofton Lee,' said Marcus. 'He came last night from the British Embassy. He is a very nice man, a great traveller. He rides on camels over the Sahara, and climbs up mountains. It is very uncomfortable and dangerous, that kind of life. I would not like it myself.'

'Oh, he's *that* man, is he?' said Crosbie. 'I've read his book.'

'I came over on the plane with him,' said Victoria.

Both men, or so it seemed to her, looked at her with interest.

'He's very pleased with himself,' said Victoria.

'I knew his aunt in India,' said Mrs Cardew Trench. 'The whole family is like that. They are terribly clever, but they can't help telling everyone.'

'Another drink?' Marcus demanded.

'Not for me,' said Victoria quickly.

Thanking Marcus for the drink, Victoria went up and lay down on her bed to do some serious thinking. How long would it be before Marcus presented her bill?

She had no idea.

When would Edward get back from Basrah? Perhaps, she thought, horrified, Edward would have forgotten all about her. Why on earth had she come rushing out to Baghdad in this silly way?

She must get a job — any job. If not, they would take her to a Consul and she would be sent back to England and never see Edward again . . .

At this point, <u>exhausted</u> from all the emotion, Victoria fell asleep.

★ ★ ★

She woke hours later and decided, 'It's no good worrying any more.' So going down to the restaurant, she ate the entire menu. When she had finished, she felt very, very full, but much happier.

Before going to bed, she went out on to the terrace. One of the waiters was standing beside the <u>railing</u>, looking down into the water. He jumped guiltily when Victoria appeared and hurried back into the hotel by the service door.

Victoria was delighted by the Tigris in the moonlight.

'Well, anyway, I've got here,' said Victoria to herself, feeling much happier, 'and I'll manage somehow. Everything will be alright in the end.'

As she went up to bed, the waiter came quietly out again and finished what he had been trying to do, which was to tie a rope so that it hung down to the river. Having done this, Mr Dakin went back into the shadows where he changed from the waiter's white coat back into his own blue suit.

Soon another man joined him. Dakin asked in a low voice, 'Everything alright?'

'Yes, sir, nothing suspicious to report,' Crosbie said quietly. 'Who's the girl?'

'She says she's the niece of the archaeologist, Pauncefoot Jones.'

'But she came on the same plane as Crofton Lee . . .'

'Yes, we must be careful,' said Dakin.

Crosbie replied, 'Do you really think it's best to move from the Embassy to here, in spite of the whole thing being planned to the smallest detail?'

'It was planned to the smallest detail in Basrah – and that ended with Salah Hassan poisoned and a shooting at the Consulate. If our plans are known, it's easy for the other side to act. I doubt

Carmichael could get near the Embassy – and even if he did . . .'
He shook his head. 'Here, only you and I and Crofton Lee know
what's going on.'

'They'll know Crofton Lee moved here from the Embassy.'

'Of course. But, Crosbie, whatever the enemy does, they've
got to do it quickly and without planning. They couldn't possibly
have put someone into the Tio six months ago – to be ready and
waiting. The Tio's never been part of the plan until now.'

He looked at his watch. 'I'll go up and see Crofton Lee now.'

Sir Rupert's door opened silently to let Dakin in. There was
only one small lamp on and the traveller had placed his chair
beside it. As he sat down again, he put a small gun onto the
table. 'What's your opinion, Dakin? Do you think Carmichael
will come?'

'Yes, Sir Rupert.' Then he said, 'You've never met him, have
you?'

'No.' Sir Rupert looked at him sharply. 'You've got the place
guarded?'

'Crosbie's on the balcony, and I shall be watching the stairs.
When Carmichael reaches you, knock on the wall and I'll
come in.'

Crofton Lee nodded.

Dakin went quietly out of the room.

Chapter 12

Victoria, having slept most of the afternoon, didn't feel sleepy at all. So she sat down and wrote several advertisements to find work; a telegram asking for help from her only living relative, a very old and unpleasant gentleman who had never helped anybody in his life; then she tried out a new hair style, and finally, with a sudden sigh, she was ready for bed.

At that moment her bedroom door opened, a man came in, locked the door and said to her urgently, 'Please, hide me – quickly.'

Victoria's reactions were never slow. In a second she had noted the painful breathing, the weak voice and the desperate way the man held an old red knitted scarf against his chest. She responded immediately to the adventure.

The bed was large – and memories of playing hide-and-seek as a child made Victoria say, 'Quick.' She pushed off the pillows, and opened the sheet and blanket. The man lay across the top of the bed. Victoria pulled the sheet and blanket over him, and put the pillows on top.

Almost immediately there was a knock at the door.

'Open the door, please. It is the police,' said a man's voice.

As Victoria crossed the room, she noticed the red knitted scarf on the floor. She picked it up and put it into a drawer, then opening the door a little, she looked out nervously.

A dark-haired young man in a striped suit was outside and behind him was a man in police uniform.

'What's the matter?' Victoria asked in alarm.

The young man smiled brightly.

'I am so sorry, miss, to trouble you at this hour, but a criminal has escaped. He has run into this hotel. We must look in every room. He is very dangerous.'

'Oh dear!' Victoria stepped back, opening the door wide. 'How frightening! Look in the bathroom, please. Oh! And the wardrobe – and under the bed! He might have been there all evening.'

The search was very quick.

'No, he is not here.'

'You're sure?'

'Thank you, miss.'

The young man <u>bowed</u> and they left.

Victoria re-locked the door and turned to the bed. She had probably been very foolish – letting her romantic nature put her on the side of the hunted against the hunter.

She said abruptly, 'They've gone. You can get up now.'

There was no movement under the pillows. Impatiently, Victoria threw them off.

The young man lay as she had left him. But now his face was grey, his eyes were closed and a bright red mark was spreading on the blanket.

'Oh, no,' said Victoria. 'Oh, no!'

The <u>wounded</u> man opened his eyes and looked at her as though from very far away.

His lips opened – the sound was so quiet that Victoria had to move very close.

'What?'

With great difficulty, the young man said two words. 'Lucifer – Basrah . . .'

His eyes closed. He said one word more. Then he lay still.

Victoria's heart was beating violently. She was filled with pity and anger.

A sound made her turn – the key had fallen out of her door. She heard the lock turning. The door opened and Mr Dakin came in, closing the door behind him.

He walked across to her, saying quietly, 'Nice work, my dear. You think quickly. How is he?'

With a break in her voice Victoria said, 'He's – he's dead.'

She saw the other's face change, saw a flash of violent anger, then it was gone – only now it seemed to her that the tiredness she had seen in his face yesterday had gone too, and that something quite different was in its place.

He gently opened the dead man's jacket.

'He was stabbed through the heart,' said Dakin as he stood up. 'Carmichael was a brave man – and a clever one.'

Victoria managed to say, 'The police came. They said he was a criminal.'

'No. He wasn't a criminal.'

'Were they really the police?'

'They may have been,' said Dakin. 'Did he say anything – before he died?'

'Yes. Lucifer – and then Basrah. And then he said – I think it was a French name – it sounded like Lefarge. What does it all mean? And what must I do?'

'I don't want you connected with this, if that's possible,' said Dakin. 'I'll come back later and tell you what it's all about. The first thing to do is to get hold of Marcus. Just do something about your appearance before I bring him in. Marcus will always help a beautiful woman in <u>distress</u>.'

He left the room. As though in a dream, Victoria combed back her hair, made up her face so it seemed white with shock, and fell on to a chair as Dakin came in. Behind him came Marcus Tio. This time there was not the usual smile on his face.

'Now, Marcus,' said Mr Dakin, 'you must do what you can about this. It's been a terrible shock to this poor girl. The man ran in – she's got a very kind heart and she hid him from the police. And now he's dead.'

'Of course she did,' said Marcus. 'Nobody likes the police. I do not like the police. But I have to keep good relations with them because of my hotel. You want me to give them money?'

'We want you to take the body away quietly.'

'That is very nice, I agree. I, too, I do not want a body in my hotel. But it is not so easy to do.'

'I think it could be,' said Dakin. 'You've got a doctor in your family, haven't you?'

'Yes, Paul, my sister's husband. But I do not want him in trouble.'

'He won't be,' said Dakin. 'Listen, Marcus. We move the body into my room. That way, Miss Jones is no longer involved. Then I use your telephone. In ten minutes a young man comes into the hotel; he is very drunk, he holds his side. He shouts for me. He walks into my room and falls. I come out and ask you for a doctor. Your brother-in-law sends for an ambulance and goes in it with this drunken friend of mine. Before they get to the hospital, my friend is dead. He has been stabbed in the street before coming into your hotel. That is all right for you.'

'And the young man who plays the drunk, he goes away quietly. And there is no body found in my hotel? And Miss Jones does not get any worry? I think, that is a very good idea.'

Chapter 13

Victoria lay in bed listening. She heard loud drunken arguing. Heard a voice insisting, 'I had a fight with a man outside.' She heard bells ring. More voices and a lot of movement. Then silence. She heard the gentle opening of her door and sat up in bed and switched on the lamp.

Dakin brought a chair up to the bed, sat down and looked at her as if he was a doctor.

'Tell me what it's all about?' demanded Victoria.

'Suppose,' said Dakin, 'that you tell me all about yourself first. Why did you come to Baghdad?'

Victoria thought afterwards that it was something in Dakin's personality, but for once she simply told him everything: her meeting with Edward, her determination to get to Baghdad and the wonderful luck of Mrs Hamilton Clipp.

'I see,' said Dakin when she had finished. 'The point is, you are involved in this whether I like it or not. So, you might as well work for me.'

'You've got a job for me?' Victoria said hopefully.

'This job, Victoria, is dangerous.'

'Oh, that's all right,' said Victoria happily. She added doubtfully, 'It's not dishonest, is it? I know I tell an awful lot of lies, but I wouldn't like to do anything dishonest.'

Dakin smiled. 'Strangely enough, your ability to invent a good lie quickly is one of your qualifications for the job. No, it's not dishonest. In fact, you will be working for law and order. Have you thought much about world politics?'

'I know everybody says there's going to be another war <u>sooner or later</u>. Between Russia and America.'

'Exactly,' said Mr Dakin. 'Therefore everything <u>depends</u> on them agreeing with each other. Instead, the opposite is happening. Every time there is a chance of agreement, something happens to create more distrust or <u>hysterical</u> fear. These things are not accidents, Victoria, they are deliberate – a group is working undercover to cause this destruction. A group that wants to take control.'

'But how do you know?'

'Money, Victoria. Money is always the clue to what is happening in the world – it's the key to any plan. A group of people are cleverly moving very large sums of money around and using that money to create <u>conflict</u>.'

'But who are these people?'

'Idealists who intend, I fear, to "make the world better"! To think that you can force "Perfection" on the human race is one of the most dangerous ideas in existence. The <u>belief</u> that some men are Supermen and therefore good enough to rule the world – that, Victoria, is the most evil of all beliefs. For when you say, "I am not like other men", you have lost the two most valuable qualities: humility and brotherhood.'

He sighed. 'Well, I mustn't <u>preach</u> a <u>sermon</u>. What we know is that in the past two years, many of the best young scientists have disappeared. The same has happened with engineers and other people with valuable skills. And we are beginning to guess what they are doing.'

Victoria listened with increasing concern.

'There is a remote part of the world, protected by mountains and deserts, that is only visited by exceptional travellers. It can be reached from China, or the Himalayas, but the journey is hard and long. Machines and people from all over the world are being sent there.

'One man followed that route. What he found was so incredible that when he got back to civilization, only two people believed his story. One was myself and, because he had been to these remote regions, the other was Sir Rupert Crofton Lee. It was from one of these journeys that Sir Rupert brought back some uranium-rich rock.

'The result was that Carmichael, a man who works for us in the intelligence service, decided to go on a desperate journey. We heard nothing for nine months, then news came. He'd got what he went to get. Proof. But the other side knew about him and their agents were already inside our whole system – some at a very high level. Somehow or other Carmichael got through safely – until tonight.'

'Then that was – the dead man in my room?'

'Yes, my dear. A very brave young man.'

'But what about the proof? Did they get it?'

A slow smile showed on Dakin's tired face. 'Knowing Carmichael, I'm sure they didn't. But he died without being able to tell us where that proof is. I think he tried to give us a clue.' He repeated slowly, 'Lucifer – Basrah – Lefarge. He'd been in Basrah – he tried to report at the Consulate and was very nearly shot. It's possible that he left the proof in Basrah. What I want you to do, Victoria, is to go there and try to find out.'

'Me? I'd love to go to Basrah,' said Victoria with enthusiasm.

Dakin smiled.

'It suits you because your young man is there, eh? What a very good reason for going there. Nothing could seem more natural. You go to Basrah and look for what Lucifer and Lefarge mean.'

'What do I use for money?' said Victoria in a business-like way. 'I did some reading on the plane and it's about three hundred and forty miles to Basrah.'

Dakin handed her a roll of paper money.

'Talk to Mrs Cardew Trench tomorrow morning, say you want to visit Basrah before you go off to this dig you're pretending to work at. She'll tell you at once that you must stay at the Consulate and will send a telegram to Mrs Clayton. You'll probably find your Edward there – everyone who passes through stays with the Claytons. Apart from that, I give you one warning. If – er – anything unpleasant happens, if you're asked what you know – don't try and be a hero. Tell them everything at once.'

'Thank you,' said Victoria. 'I'm rather afraid of pain, and if anyone were to <u>torture</u> me, I'm afraid I wouldn't be brave.'

'They won't torture you,' said Mr Dakin. 'Torture's very old-fashioned. They'll put a drug in your arm and you'll answer every question truthfully. That's why I didn't want you to get grand ideas of secrecy.'

'What about Edward? Do I tell him?'

Dakin thought for a moment.

'That would put him in danger, too. But I understand he had a good record in the Air Force. I don't suppose danger will worry him. Two heads are often better than one. And he thinks there's something suspicious about this "Olive Branch" he's working for. That's interesting.'

'Why?'

'Because we think so too,' said Dakin.

Then he added, 'And keep your ears open for any mention of a young woman called Anna Scheele. We would really like to know much more about her.'

Chapter 14

A car met Victoria at the station, she was driven to the Consulate and in through big gates into a delightful garden. The car stopped in front of steps leading up to a balcony surrounding the house. Mrs Clayton, a smiling energetic woman, came through a door at the top of the steps to meet her.

'We're so pleased to see you,' she said. 'Basrah's really delightful at this time of year, though there's no one here now except Dr Rathbone's young man who's quite charming. What would you like first – a bath or some coffee?'

'A bath, please,' said Victoria gratefully.

If possible, Victoria hoped to meet Edward alone. With this in mind, when she had bathed and put on a summer dress, she went quietly out to sit on the balcony.

The first to arrive was a tall thin man with a thoughtful face, and as he came up the steps, Victoria went to stand out of sight round the corner of the balcony. As she did so, she saw Edward entering through a garden gate that opened on to the river.

Victoria called out quietly. 'Up here.'

Edward, who was, Victoria thought, more attractive than ever, turned quickly – and complete surprise appeared on his face.

'My goodness! Victoria!'

'Quiet. Wait for me. I'm coming down.'

Victoria ran round the balcony, down the steps and along to where Edward stood, confusion still on his face.

'I can't be drunk so early in the day,' said Edward. 'It *is* you.'

'Yes, it's me,' said Victoria happily.

'But . . . it's unbelievable. How did you get here?'

'I flew.'

'I mean, what wonderful chance brought you to Basrah?'

'The train,' said Victoria.

'You're doing it on purpose, you little witch. I am so pleased to see you. But how did you get here – really?'

'I came out with an American woman who'd broken her arm. I was offered the job the day after I met you, and you'd talked about Baghdad, so I thought, why not see the world?'

'You really are great fun, Victoria. But what are you doing now?'

'I'm still seeing the world,' said Victoria. 'But I've had to do a few tricks. The idea is that I am Miss Pauncefoot Jones. My uncle is a famous archaeologist who is working out here, and I am joining him soon.'

'Oh, excellent, that's a good story. But what will happen if you and Jones come face to face?'

'I don't think that is likely. From what I hear, once archaeologists start to dig, they go on digging like mad, and don't stop.'

'I say, you really are wonderful, Victoria!' said Edward admiringly. 'I've never met anyone like you.'

Edward's admiring look caused Victoria great satisfaction. If she had been a cat, she would have purred.

'And you will actually want a job, won't you?' said Edward.

'Yes,' said Victoria, 'I actually went into your Olive Branch and asked Dr Rathbone for a job, but he wasn't helpful.'

'The old man is tight with his money,' said Edward. 'He wants everybody to work for love.'

'Do you think he's a <u>fake</u>, Edward?'

'I don't know exactly what I think. He doesn't make any money. So far as I can see, all that enthusiasm is real. And yet, you know, I don't believe he's a fool.'

'We'd better go in,' said Victoria. 'We can talk later.'

★ ★ ★

'I'd no idea you and Edward knew each other,' said Mrs Clayton.

'Oh, we're old friends,' laughed Victoria. 'Only we'd lost contact. I'd no idea Edward was here.'

Mr Clayton, who was the man Victoria had seen coming up the steps, asked, 'How did you get on this morning, Edward? Any progress?'

'Oh, the books are there, sir, but the forms to get them are unending. The person you need always seems to be away that day. Everyone is very willing – only nothing seems to happen.'

Everyone laughed and Mrs Clayton said, 'You'll get them in the end. It was very wise of Dr Rathbone to send someone down personally.'

As everything was closed during the midday hours, Edward and Victoria went out after lunch to see the sights. Victoria was delighted with the Shatt el Arab River, and the palm trees beside it. She loved the Arab boats tied up in the canal in the town. They walked slowly into the souk. When they turned towards the Consulate and Edward was preparing to leave for work, Victoria asked suddenly, 'Edward, what's your last name? I don't know it.'

Edward <u>stared</u> at her.

'Don't you? No, I suppose you don't. It's Goring.'

'Edward Goring. You've no idea what a fool I felt going into that Olive Branch place and wanting to ask for you and not knowing anything but Edward.'

'Was there a dark-skinned girl there? With rather long hair?'

'Yes.'

'That's Catherine. If you said "Edward", she'd know.'

'I am sure she would,' said Victoria without enthusiasm.

'She's a very nice girl. Didn't you think so?'

'Oh ...'

'Very kind.'

'Is she?' Victoria's voice was now as cold as ice – but Edward did not seem to notice.

'I don't know what I would have done without her. I'm sure you and she will be great friends.'

'I don't think we'll have the chance.'

'Oh yes, you will. I'm going to get you a job there.'

'How are you going to manage that?'

'I don't know but I shall manage it somehow. If not, next thing I know, you'll be heading for Burma. No, young Victoria, I'm not going to take any chances, I don't want you running away from me. You're too fond of seeing the world.'

'You sweet fool,' thought Victoria to herself, 'don't you know that nothing would drive me away from Baghdad now!'

Aloud she said, 'Well, it would be fun to have a job at the Olive Branch.'

'I wouldn't describe it as fun. The organization means well, but it's all a bit silly too.'

'And do you still think there's something wrong about it?'

'Oh, that was only a wild idea of mine.'

'No,' said Victoria thoughtfully, 'I think it's true.'

Edward turned on her quickly. 'What makes you say that?'

'Something I heard – from a friend of mine.'

'Who was it?'

'Just a friend.'

'Girls like you have too many friends,' Edward complained. 'You are a devil, Victoria. I love you madly and you don't care a bit.'

'Oh yes, I do,' said Victoria. 'Just a little bit.'

Then, hiding her delighted satisfaction, she asked, 'Edward, is there anyone called Lefarge connected with the Olive Branch?'

'Lefarge?' Edward looked doubtful. 'No, I don't think so.'

'Or anyone called Anna Scheele?'

This time Edward's reaction was very different. He caught her arm, 'What do you know about Anna Scheele?'

'Ow! Edward, let go! I don't know anything about her. I just wanted to know if you did.'

'Where did you hear about her? What made you think this Anna Scheele had anything to do with the Olive Branch?'

'Has she?'

Edward said slowly, 'I don't know. It's all so – so unclear.' He looked at his watch. 'I must go,' he said. 'But we've got to get together, Victoria. There's a lot I want to know.'

★ ★ ★

That evening Edward and Victoria walked together in the Consulate garden. The sunset was beautiful but neither of the young people noticed it.

'It began simply,' said Victoria, 'with a man coming into my room at the Tio Hotel and getting stabbed.'

It was not, perhaps, most people's idea of a simple beginning. Edward said, 'Getting what?'

'Stabbed,' said Victoria. 'Anyway,' she added, 'he was dead.'

'How could he come into your room if he was dead?'

'Oh Edward, don't be stupid.'

For some mysterious reason Victoria could never tell the truth in a simple way. Her story was uncertain and incomplete and it sounded as if she was telling a terrible lie.

When she came to the end, Edward looked at her doubtfully and said, 'You do feel alright, Victoria, don't you? I mean you haven't had a dream, or anything?'

'Of course not.'

'Because, I mean, it seems such an impossible thing to have happened.'

'Well, it did happen,' Victoria insisted.

'And all that dramatic stuff about world powers and mysterious secrets, things like that simply don't happen. Honest, Victoria – are you <u>making</u> this <u>up</u>?'

'No!' cried Victoria annoyed.

'And you've come down here looking for someone called Lefarge and someone called Anna Scheele . . .'

'Whom you've heard of,' Victoria added.

'Yes . . . but I don't know if it means anything. It was just – odd. You see, Victoria, I'm not as clever as you. You see things and you understand what those things mean. I just sort of feel that things are – well – wrong – but I don't know why.'

'I feel like that sometimes, too,' said Victoria. 'Like seeing Sir Rupert on the balcony of the Tio Hotel.'

'Who's Sir Rupert?'

'Sir Rupert Crofton Lee. He was on the plane coming out. A famous man. And when I saw him sitting on the balcony at the Tio, I had that strange feeling, like you've just said, that something was wrong, but I didn't know what it was.'

'Rathbone asked him to come and give a talk at the Olive Branch, I believe, but he couldn't come.'

'Well, go on about Anna Scheele.'

'Oh, Anna Scheele. It was one of the girls.'

'Catherine?' said Victoria immediately.

'I believe it was, now I think of it. Well, Catherine said to one of the other girls, "When Anna Scheele comes, we can move forward. Then we'll get our orders from her – and her alone".'

'That's really important, Edward. Didn't you think it was strange at the time?'

'No, of course I didn't. I thought it was just some woman who was coming out – perhaps a new boss. Are you sure you're not imagining all this, Victoria?'

As soon as he saw the look his young friend gave him, he was immediately sorry.

'All right, all right,' he said quickly. 'Only, you'll admit, the whole story just doesn't seem real. And you are very good at making things up. The Bishop of Llangow and all that!'

'Oh, that was just girlish fun,' said Victoria. 'This is serious. But look here, Edward, how do you know . . .?'

A call from the balcony interrupted her.

'Come in, you two - drinks waiting.'

'Coming,' called Victoria.

★ ★ ★

Victoria went to bed that night with strangely mixed feelings. Her journey had ended – and she had found Edward! Then she shuddered. In spite of everything, she had a feeling of disappointment.

Words floated through her head. Something she had meant to ask Edward in the garden – but Mrs Clayton had called and it had gone out of her head. She must remember because it was important; something was wrong. If only she could remember before sleep . . .

Victoria dreamed. She dreamed of a woman coming towards her along a hotel corridor – it was herself – but when the woman got near, she saw the face was Catherine's. Edward and Catherine – how silly!

'Come with me,' she said to Edward, 'we will find Mr Lefarge . . .'

And suddenly Edward had gone and she was alone in the dark with evil all around her. And she was holding a brown coat, covered with blood. She was running in terror down a hotel corridor. And they were coming after her.

Victoria woke suddenly from her dream, her heart beating wildly.

Chapter 15

'You found your young man?' asked Mr Dakin.

Victoria nodded. 'Yes, and Edward thinks he can get me a job at the Olive Branch. And they know something about Anna Scheele there.' Victoria repeated what Edward had told her.

'Now that's very interesting,' said Mr Dakin.

'Who is Anna Scheele?' asked Victoria.

'She's secretary to the head of an international bank. She disappeared in London about ten days ago.'

'Is she coming to Baghdad?'

'If we can believe this young woman Catherine, then yes, she is,' Mr Dakin said thoughtfully.

'Perhaps I can find out more at the Olive Branch.'

'Perhaps – but be very careful, Victoria. I would prefer not to have your body floating in the river.'

Victoria shuddered, 'Like Sir Rupert Crofton Lee's? That was horrible. Mrs Clayton got the awful news at breakfast – that's when we heard it. A report from Cairo announcing that the body of Sir Rupert has been taken out of the Nile. First Carmichael and now Sir Rupert. All the people who know about this business are being killed. You know, that morning when Sir Rupert was here at the hotel, there was something strange about him.'

'In what way – strange?'

'Well – different.' She shook her head, annoyed. 'I will remember it sometime. Anyway. There is something I want to ask you. Who stabbed Carmichael? Was it someone who followed him here?'

'No,' said Dakin slowly. 'He came in one of those Arab boats – and he wasn't followed. I had someone watching the river.'

'Then it was someone – in the hotel?'

'Yes, I was watching the stairs and no one came up. Yet all the people in the hotel are unlikely for one very good reason.'

'What is that?'

'Carmichael was <u>on his guard</u>. He had a very strong <u>instinct</u> for danger. So he must have been stabbed by someone he trusted.'

★ ★ ★

Somehow, Edward had <u>persuaded</u> Dr Rathbone to offer Victoria a very low-paid job. She spent most of her time typing – or encouraging good feeling amongst visitors who mostly looked at one another with dislike. The Olive Branch was full of that sort of international peace. The meetings were held with orange juice to drink and boring food to go with it. As far as Victoria could see, everything was respectable and very dull.

She was now living with some other young female workers in a house by the river. It seemed to Victoria that Catherine watched her in an unfriendly way – it was known that Edward had helped Victoria get her job and several pairs of jealous eyes looked at her unkindly.

Though the Olive Branch seemed respectable, Victoria had a strong feeling that Dr Rathbone was not. Once or twice she noticed his dark eyes looking at her and though she returned her most innocent and sweet expression, she felt a sudden shock of fear.

She rarely saw Edward since he was always being sent to far-off places by Dr Rathbone – he had only just come back from Iran.

'Really,' thought Victoria, 'I see so little of Edward, I might as well have stayed in England!'

Soon afterwards, however, Edward brought her some papers. 'Dr Rathbone would like these typed at once, please, Victoria.'

A tiny note in Edward's handwriting was pinned to the top sheet.

The Tigris riverbank, past the House of King Ali, tomorrow morning about eleven.

The following day was Friday, the weekly holiday. Victoria's spirits rose high. She really must get her hair washed.

'It really needs it,' she said aloud.

'What did you say?' Catherine, at work on a pile of leaflets, raised her head suspiciously from the next table.

Victoria said, 'My hair needs washing. Most of these hairdressing places look so dirty, I don't know where to go.'

'Yes, they are dirty. But I know a girl who washes hair very well and the towels are clean. I will take you there.'

'That's very kind of you, Catherine.'

'We will go tomorrow.'

'Thank you,' said Victoria. 'That's very kind. But not tomorrow.'

Chapter 16

The old car bumped madly over the rough road. The driver turned and smiled at them.

'Where are we going?'

'To Babylon,' said Edward. 'It's time we had a day out.'

'To Babylon?' cried Victoria. 'How lovely. Really, to Babylon?'

'Yes, but don't expect too much. Babylon isn't as impressive as it was.'

'The road isn't very good, is it?' gasped Victoria, bouncing in her seat.

'It gets worse later on,' said Edward.

They bounced along happily. The dust rose in clouds. Large lorries full of Arabs raced along in the middle of the road, paying no attention to the other drivers. They passed walled gardens and groups of women and children and donkeys – and to Victoria it was all delightful.

They reached Babylon in two hours and were happy to get out of the car. The pile of mud and ruins was a disappointment to Victoria, who had expected columns and arches.

But her disappointment disappeared as their guide led them along the Processional Way to the Ishtar Gate, with their pictures of unbelievable animals high on the walls. A sudden sense of a grand history came to Victoria and a wish to know something about this huge, proud city that now lay dead and empty.

After a while, they sat down by the Babylonian Lion to eat the picnic lunch that Edward had brought. The guide moved away, smiling and telling them firmly that they must see the museum later.

'Must we?' said Victoria dreamily. 'Things in glass cases don't seem real somehow. I went to the British Museum once. It was very tiring for the feet.'

'The past is always boring,' said Edward. 'The future's much more important.'

'This isn't boring,' said Victoria, waving a sandwich towards the ruins. 'There's a feeling of – of greatness here. A city of great Kings. Would you have liked to be a King of Babylon, Edward?'

Edward took a deep breath. 'Yes, I would. They understood how to be Kings in those days! That's why they could rule the world and put everything in order.'

How strange, thought Victoria, to be sitting in the ruins of Babylon talking like this. The sun was very hot and bright, and the ruins were pale and <u>shimmering</u> in the heat, with a background of dark palm trees. How very nicely Edward's hair grew down, with a little curl into his neck, Victoria found herself thinking. And what a nice neck – brown from the sun with no marks on it –

Suddenly Victoria sat up straight, wildly excited.

'I've just remembered, about Sir Rupert Crofton Lee.'

Edward looked at her blankly.

'He sat in front of me in the plane and I saw it – a boil on his neck.'

'Why shouldn't he have a boil? Painful, but lots of people get them.'

'Yes, yes, of course. But the point is that morning on the balcony he didn't have one.'

'One what?'

'A boil. Oh, Edward, do try and understand! In the aeroplane he had a boil and on the balcony at the Tio, he didn't. His neck was unmarked. So you see what it means – the man at the Tio wasn't Sir Rupert.'

She nodded violently. Edward stared at her.

'You're mad, Victoria. It must have been Sir Rupert.'

'No. Don't you see, Edward, I never looked at him properly, only at the general effect: the hat, the cloak, the whole appearance. How easy to copy that!'

'But why . . .'

'Because of Carmichael, of course. Carmichael was coming to Baghdad to tell him what he had discovered. And Carmichael wouldn't be on his guard with him. Of course – it was the false Rupert Crofton Lee who stabbed Carmichael!'

'I don't believe a word of it. It's madness. Don't forget, Sir Rupert was killed too, afterwards in Cairo.'

'Oh Edward, how awful! I saw it happen.'

'You saw it happen – Victoria, are you completely mad?'

'No, not at all. Just listen, Edward. There was a knock on my door – in the hotel in Cairo – at least I thought it was on my door and I looked out, but it was actually next door to mine, on Sir Rupert Crofton Lee's. It was one of the air hostesses. She asked him if he could go to the BOAC office. Don't you see, Edward? It was a trap, an impersonator was waiting, all ready, and as soon as Sir Rupert went into the office, they hit him on the head and the other man came out and took his place. They killed the real Sir Rupert when the impersonator came back to Cairo.'

'It's a wonderful story,' said Edward. 'But you know, Victoria, there is no evidence.'

'There's the boil . . .'

'Oh, forget the boil!'

'And there are one or two other things.'

'What?'

'The BOAC notice on the door. It wasn't there later. I remembered being surprised when I found the BOAC office was on the other side of the building. And the air stewardess. I've seen her since – here in Baghdad – at the Olive Branch. The first day I went there. She came in and spoke to Catherine. I thought then that I'd seen her before.'

After a silence, Edward said slowly, 'It all comes back to the Olive Branch – and to Catherine. Victoria, you've got to get closer to Catherine. Be nice to her. Somehow or other get to know who her friends are and where she goes and who she meets outside the Olive Branch.'

'What about Mr Dakin?' asked Victoria. 'Ought I to tell him about this?'

'Yes, of course. But wait a day or two. We may have a lot more to tell him.'

★ ★ ★

Excited by her discoveries, Victoria found it easy to speak to Catherine kindly the following day. When they left the Olive Branch together that evening, the two girls were much more like friends. Catherine led her in and out of narrow alleys and finally knocked on a door where a young woman welcomed them in English. She invited Victoria to sit by a clean <u>basin</u>, with shining taps and bottles of shampoo placed round it. Catherine left and Victoria relaxed in the care of an expert hairdresser. Soon her hair was covered in lovely creamy shampoo.

'And now, please . . .' said the young hairdresser.

Victoria moved her head over the basin. Water flowed over her hair and suddenly there was a sweet, sickly, hospital smell. A wet cloth was pressed over her nose and mouth. She fought wildly, but her thoughts were losing focus, a loud noise filled her ears . . .

Then blackness.

Chapter 17

Victoria woke with confused memories – a bumping car – Arabs arguing – a horrible feeling that she would be sick – then she remembered lying on a bed and an injection – then more darkness.

Something had happened – that horrible smell – <u>chloroform</u>, of course. And then a sleeping drug.

Well, they hadn't killed her. So that was all right. She was lying on a hard bed in a small room with a floor of hard earth. There was an old table with a basin on it and a <u>bucket</u> underneath it – and a window with wooden bars outside.

Victoria got off the bed slowly, feeling headachy, and went to the window. She could see through the bars into a garden with palm trees beyond it. She turned to the door, which was large and locked.

She went back and sat on the bed.

Where was she? Not in Baghdad, that was certain. And what was she going to do next? Even more important, what was someone going to do to her?

She heard footsteps and then there was the noise of a very large key in an old lock. The door opened slowly. An Arab carried in a tray.

He spoke some Arabic, put down the tray and left, locking the door behind him.

On the tray was a large bowl of rice, some cabbage leaves and a big piece of Arab bread – also a jug of water and a glass.

Victoria drank some water and then started eating hungrily. When she had finished everything, she felt much better.

She also felt that it would be much better if by tomorrow she was somewhere else. But was that possible? She went to examine the door, but there was nothing she could do. This wasn't the kind of lock you could open easily.

The window – she could break the wooden bars. But the noise would attract attention.

'<u>Damn</u>,' said Victoria.

She approached the old table for another drink of water – and some fell on the floor. At once it turned into mud. An idea formed in Miss Victoria Jones' always active brain.

The sun was setting. Very soon it would be dark. What she needed was something to push with. She looked round. On the table was a large spoon. That might be useful. She went back to the door and pushed vigorously through the large keyhole until the key fell out.

'Now,' Victoria thought, 'I must hurry, before the light goes completely.' She picked up the jug of water and poured some at the bottom of the door near where she thought the key had fallen on the other side. Then, using the spoon, she began to dig out the wet part. Little by little, pouring more water, she dug a hole under the door. Lying down, she could get her arm through it. She felt about and found the key, pulling it back to her side of the door.

Holding the key in her muddy hand, Victoria waited until some dogs started barking loudly, then she turned the key in the lock. The door opened, showing her another room – with an open door at the other end. It led out to the garden.

A piece of ragged black material lay near the outside door. It was an old *aba*, the large, loose dress that Arab women wore. It would be useful for covering her Western clothes. Victoria would wait until the village went to sleep and then she would go.

It seemed to Victoria that she waited for hours but at last the human noises stopped. She heard only the distant barking of dogs. The moon was low in the sky. It gave enough light to see her way to the opening in the mud wall around the garden. She walked quickly through some trees and came out into an alley between mud-brick walls. Victoria ran along it as fast as she could.

Now dogs began to bark loudly. Victoria turned a corner and came into the main street. Narrow and rough, it ran through a village of mud-brick houses, all pale in the moonlight. Palms hung over walls, dogs barked.

Victoria ran.

Soon she came out to a muddy river with an old stone bridge over it – and a <u>track</u> heading out into the desert. Victoria ran until she was out of breath.

The village was far behind her now. The moon was high. To her left and right and front was open stony ground without any sign of people. And Victoria had no idea in what direction the track led. But it was impossible to turn back.

She started walking towards the unknown.

Morning came at last. Victoria was exhausted and her feet were sore. She saw that she was heading southwest, and to the side of the road ahead of her was a low, flat-topped hill. Victoria left the track and went towards it, climbing to the top.

With a feeling of panic she looked at the country all around. Everywhere there was nothing. The scene was beautiful in the early morning light. The ground and horizon were coloured with faint shades of orange and cream on which were patterns of shadows. It was beautiful, but frightening.

'I know what it means now,' thought Victoria, 'when someone says they are alone in the world.'

Suddenly she heard a car. It was coming towards the village – so it was not someone chasing her. It was still only a small black dot far off on the track.

But suppose this was the enemy?

Victoria went down the hill as quickly as she could and then lay down. She watched the car come nearer. There was an Arab driver and beside him a man in European clothes.

'Now,' thought Victoria, 'I've got to decide.'

Should she stop the car?

How could she be sure? The track was deserted. Nothing had passed – not even a donkey. Perhaps this car was going to the village she had left last night?

If it was the enemy, it was the end. But it might be her only hope of survival.

What should she do?

As she lay there considering, the car slowed, then it came off the road towards the hill.

It had seen her!

Victoria crawled round the back of the hill. She heard the car stop and the bang of a door. Then somebody said something in Arabic. Suddenly a man came into view. He was walking round the hill, half-way up. His eyes were on the ground and from time to time he bent down and picked something up. Whatever he was looking for, it was not a girl called Victoria Jones. And even better, he was definitely an Englishman.

With a cry of relief, Victoria stood up. He lifted his head and looked at her in surprise.

'I'm so glad you've come.' said Victoria.

He still stared.

'Who on earth . . .?' he began. 'Are you English? But . . .'

With a little laugh, Victoria threw off the old *aba*.

'Of course I'm English,' she said. 'And please, can you take me back to Baghdad?'

'I'm not going to Baghdad. I've just come from there. What on earth are you doing alone out here in the middle of the desert?'

'I was <u>kidnapped</u>,' said Victoria quickly. 'I went to have my hair shampooed and they gave me chloroform. And when I woke up, I was in an Arab house in a village over there.' She pointed towards the horizon.

'In Mandali?'

'I don't know its name. I escaped and walked all through the night and then I hid behind this hill in case you were an enemy.'

Her rescuer was staring at her with a very strange expression. He was a man of about thirty five, fair-haired, with a sort of superior expression. He was very polite and correct. He now put on a pair of glasses and stared at her through them in a very superior way. Victoria decided that this man did not believe a word she was saying.

She was immediately extremely angry.

'It's perfectly true,' she said. 'Every word of it!'

The stranger looked more disbelieving than ever. 'Incredible,' he said coldly.

Victoria was frustrated. How unfair it was that she could always make a lie sound believable, but when telling the truth she didn't have the power to make people believe her.

'Well, if you haven't got anything to drink with you, I shall die of thirst,' she said.

'Abdul,' the stranger called.

'Sahib?'

The driver appeared and was sent for a large bottle of water. Victoria drank thankfully. 'Oh!' she said. 'That's better.'

'My name's Richard Baker,' said the Englishman.

'I'm Victoria Jones.' And then, in an effort to change the disbelief she saw into respectful attention, she added, 'I'm joining my uncle, Dr Pauncefoot Jones, on his dig.'

'How amazing!' said Baker. 'I'm on my way to the dig myself. It's only about fifteen miles from here. I'm just the right person to have rescued you, aren't I?'

Victoria was completely shocked – quite unable to say another word. Silently she followed Richard to the car.

'I suppose you're the <u>anthropologist</u>,' said Richard, as she sat down in the back seat. 'I didn't expect you so soon.'

He stood for a moment sorting through various pieces of broken <u>pottery</u> which he removed from his pockets. Victoria now realized that this was what he had been picking up on the hill.

'Most of it is late Assyrian,' he said, pointing towards the hill. He smiled as he added, 'I'm glad to see that in spite of your troubles your archaeological instincts led you to examine a tell.'

Victoria opened her mouth and then shut it again.

What, after all, could she say?

Fortunately, for a short time she had been a typist at the Archaeological Institute in London. So at least she knew that a tell was a hill made by people rebuilding their houses again and again in the same place. They just <u>levelled</u> the ruins of old buildings and built on top of them. Over time this made a special kind of hill. So when people like Richard Baker dug into a tell, the deeper they dug, the older the buildings they discovered.

It was also true that he would discover she was a liar as soon as they reached the dig. But it would be much, much better to be sorry there, than to confess the truth to Mr Richard Baker in the middle of nowhere. 'And, anyway,' thought Victoria, 'perhaps before I get there, I will have thought of something.'

Her busy imagination got to work immediately.

After a while Mr Baker said something to Abdul and the car turned off the track and into the desert. With nothing to guide him, as far as Victoria could see, Richard Baker directed

Abdul. Soon Richard said with satisfaction, 'Going the right way now.'

Victoria could not see any way at all. But sometimes she saw <u>vague</u> tyre marks. Then they crossed a slightly clearer collection of tyre marks and Richard called out for Abdul to stop.

'Here's an interesting sight for you,' he said to Victoria.

Two men were coming towards them. One man carried a short wooden seat, the other a big round wooden object.

They welcomed Richard warmly. He produced cigarettes and soon a party atmosphere developed.

Then Richard turned to her. 'Do you like the cinema? Then you shall see a performance.'

He spoke to the men and they smiled with pleasure. They set up the seat for Victoria and Richard to sit on. Then they set up the round wooden box on a stand. It had two little holes covered with glass and as Victoria put her eyes to them, one man began to turn a <u>handle</u>, and the other began to sing.

Richard translated, 'Come near and prepare yourself for much delight. Prepare to see ancient wonders.'

Victoria could see a coloured picture. 'The wife of the great <u>Shah</u> of the Western world,' said Richard. Then the <u>Empress</u> Eugenie touched one of her long curls; next came a picture of the King's Palace in Montenegro, another of the Great Exhibition. A strange collection of pictures followed, all different and sometimes announced with the strangest of descriptions. People skating on ice completed this strange collection of old photographs.

When the show ended, Victoria smiled with pleasure. 'That was marvellous!'

The owners of the travelling cinema smiled proudly. Richard gave them some money. Richard and Victoria got into the car and calling goodbye to them, the men walked away into the desert.

'Where are they going?' asked Victoria.

'To Kerbela, but they travel all over the country. I first met them coming up the road from the Dead Sea.'

The car still appeared to be going nowhere with complete confidence.

'Where are we going?' Victoria asked.

'To the dig at Tell Aswad. You'll see it soon. But now, look over to your left.'

'Are they clouds?' asked Victoria. 'They can't be mountains.'

'Ah, but they are. The snow-covered mountains of Kurdistan.'

A great feeling of contentment came over Victoria. If only she could drive on like this forever. If only she wasn't such a terrible liar. She felt as nervous as a child at the thought of the unpleasant meeting ahead.

'There you are,' said Richard.

Victoria could just see a small shape on the far horizon. The small shape developed very quickly into a very large tell. On one side of this great hill was a long, low building of mud-brick.

'This is where we archaeologists stay,' said Richard.

They stopped the car in the middle of a group of barking dogs. Servants in white clothes rushed out with welcoming smiles.

After an exchange of greetings in Arabic, Richard explained, 'They weren't expecting you so soon. But they'll get your bed ready. And bring you some hot water. I expect you'd like to have a wash and a rest? Dr Pauncefoot Jones is up on the tell. I'm going up to him. Ibrahim will look after you.'

He walked away and Victoria followed Ibrahim into the house. It seemed dark at first, coming in out of the sun. They passed through a living-room with some big tables and a few old armchairs, then round a courtyard and into a small room with one window. There was a bed, a chest of drawers, a chair and a table with a jug and basin on it. Ibrahim, smiling and nodding, brought her a large jug of hot water, a towel and a small mirror which he fixed to a nail on the wall.

Victoria was beginning to think how tired she was and how very dirty.

'I suppose I look terrible,' she said to herself and went to the mirror.

For some moments she stared at her reflection without understanding.

This was not Victoria Jones.

Though her features were the small neat features of Victoria Jones, her hair was now platinum blonde!

Chapter 18

Richard found Dr Pauncefoot Jones at the dig on his knees, carefully using a small tool on a length of wall.

'Hello Richard, my boy. I thought you were arriving on Tuesday.'

'This is Tuesday,' said Richard.

'Is it really now?' said Dr Pauncefoot Jones without interest. 'Just come down here and see what you think of this. Perfectly good walls are coming out already and we're only down three feet. It looks very promising.'

Richard jumped down into the long hole and the two archaeologists enjoyed themselves in a highly technical manner for a quarter of an hour.

'By the way,' said Richard, 'I've brought a girl. Says she's your niece.'

With an effort Dr Pauncefoot Jones brought his mind back from mud-brick walls.

'I don't think I have a niece,' he said doubtfully.

'She's coming to work here, I understand.'

'Oh.' Dr Pauncefoot Jones' face relaxed. 'Of course. That will be Venetia.'

'Victoria, she said.'

'Yes, yes, Victoria. A very able girl, I understand. An anthropologist. There's nothing for her yet. Of course, we're only just beginning. Actually I understood she wasn't coming for another two weeks, but I didn't read her letter very carefully, and then I lost it. My wife arrives next week – or the week after – and I thought Venetia was coming out with her. Well, well, I am sure we can make her useful. There's a lot of pottery coming up.'

'There's nothing strange about her, is there?'

'Strange?' Dr Pauncefoot Jones looked closely at him. 'In what way?'

'Well, she told me the most extraordinary story. She said she'd gone to have her hair shampooed and they chloroformed her and carried her off to Mandali and imprisoned her and she'd escaped in the middle of the night – the silliest nonsense you ever heard. She's obviously one of those very emotional girls.'

'Oh, I expect she'll calm down,' said Dr Pauncefoot Jones without concern. 'Where is she now?'

'I left her to have a wash.' He hesitated. 'She hasn't got any luggage with her.'

'Hasn't she? That is difficult. You don't think she'll expect me to lend her pyjamas? I've only got two pairs and one of them is torn.'

* * *

Victoria, waiting nervously, saw that Dr Pauncefoot Jones was a small, round man with a twinkle in his eye. To her confusion he came towards her with open arms.

'Well, well, Venetia – I mean Victoria. This is a surprise. I didn't think you were arriving until next month. But I'm delighted to see you. Delighted.'

Victoria recovered quickly, which wasn't easy.

'Richard tells me your luggage is lost,' said Dr Pauncefoot Jones. 'How are you going to manage? We can't send the lorry in to town before next week?'

'I can manage,' said Victoria, smiling.

'No signs of any human bones for you,' Dr Pauncefoot Jones warned her. 'Some nice walls are coming up – and lots of pottery. We'll keep you busy. I forget if you do photography?'

'I know something about it,' said Victoria, happy at the mention of something that she did in fact know how to do.

'Good, good. That's a help. Though the laboratory is rather basic.'

'I don't mind,' said Victoria.

She was still trying to understand it all. Clearly he thought she was an anthropologist called Venetia who was joining the expedition. Very well then, until the lorry went into Baghdad, Victoria would try to be Venetia. But she would have to be very careful. Luckily, thought Victoria, men were always so superior about women that any mistake she made would be treated as proof of how silly women were!

And spending time here would give her a rest, which she very much needed. She had hated the horrible fight against the chloroform, and she had been very frightened waking up in that room. Here, she would be well hidden. Richard's car had not passed through Mandali, so nobody could guess she was now at Tell Aswad. No, from the enemy point of view, Victoria would have disappeared. They might decide that she had got lost in the desert and died.

Well, let them think so. Unhappily, of course, Edward would think so, too! Very well, Edward must suffer. In fact he would not have to suffer long before she was back from the dead – only as a blonde instead of a <u>brunette</u>.

And that brought her back to the mystery of why they – whoever they were – had dyed her hair. There must be some reason.

'Never mind,' thought Victoria, 'I'm alive. And I will enjoy myself for a week. It will be great fun to be on an archaeological dig and see what it is like.'

She did not find it easy. The names of people, of publications, the styles of architecture and types of pottery had to be treated carefully. Fortunately a good listener is always popular. Victoria was an excellent listener and she began to learn the technical language.

She read all the time she was alone in the house. There was a good library of archaeological books and magazines. And, unexpectedly, she found the life very enjoyable. Tea was brought to her in the early morning, then she went out on the dig to help Richard with camera work. To put pottery back together. To watch as the walls of a palace were slowly dug out. To see how carefully the men worked.

Richard Baker still looked at her thoughtfully sometimes, but he was friendly and amused by her enthusiasm.

'It's all new to you,' he said one day. 'I remember how excited I was my first season.'

'How long ago was that?'

He smiled. 'Rather a long time ago – fifteen years.'

'You talk Arabic very well. If you were dressed as one, could you pass as an Arab?'

He shook his head. 'Oh no! The only man I know who could pass as one is a man who was actually born here. His father was Consul in lots of wild places. We were at school together. In fact, I saw him only the other day at Basrah. First time in years – and in rather strange <u>circumstances</u>.'

'Strange?'

'Yes. I didn't recognize him. He was dressed as an Arab, with a string of those beads they carry and he started making little clicking noises with it – only, you see, he was actually using Morse code. He was clicking out a message – to me!'

'What did it say?'

'My school nickname and his, then he made a signal to expect trouble.'

'And was there trouble?'

'Yes. An Englishman with a gun. I knocked his arm up – and Carmichael got away.'

'Carmichael?'

He turned his head quickly.

'Do you know him?'

'Yes,' she said. 'I knew him.'

'Knew him? Why – is he . . .'

Victoria nodded. 'Yes. He's dead. He was killed in Baghdad. In the Tio Hotel. It was kept quiet. Nobody knows.'

He nodded slowly. 'I see. It was that kind of business. But you . . .' He looked at her. 'How did you know?'

'I got mixed up in it – by accident.'

He gave her a long considering look.

Victoria asked suddenly, 'Your nickname at school wasn't Lucifer, was it?'

He looked surprised. 'Lucifer, no? I was Owl – because I had to wear glasses.'

'You don't know anyone who is called Lucifer – in Basrah?'

Richard shook his head. 'Lucifer, Son of the Morning – the fallen angel.' He watched her closely as he spoke, but Victoria was frowning.

'Where were you when all this happened at Basrah?' she asked.

'It was in the waiting room of the Consulate. There were a couple of others and this Englishman and Carmichael.'

'And you stopped the man with the gun and Carmichael got out – how?'

'He turned first towards the Consul's office. It's at the other end of a passage with a garden . . .'

She interrupted. 'I know. I stayed there for a day or two.'

Once again he watched her closely – but Victoria didn't notice. She was seeing the long passage at the Consulate, with the door opening on to green trees and sunlight.

'Well, Carmichael went that way first. Then he turned and ran the other way into the street.'

'What about the Englishman?'

Richard shook his head. 'He told some story about having been robbed by an Arab. I didn't hear any more because I flew on to Kuwait.'

'Who was staying at the Consulate just then?' Victoria asked.

'A man called Crosbie – one of the oil people. Oh yes, I believe there was someone else from Baghdad, but I didn't meet him. I can't remember his name.'

Victoria remembered Captain Crosbie – and that he had been back in Baghdad the night Carmichael came to the Tio Hotel. Could Carmichael have seen Crosbie at the end of the passage, standing against the sunlight? Was that why he had turned and run towards the street, instead of trying to reach the Consul-General's office?

She jumped rather guiltily when she looked up to find Richard Baker watching her closely.

'Any more questions?'

'Do you know anybody called Lefarge?' Victoria asked.

'No. Man or woman?'

'I don't know.'

She was wondering about Crosbie.

Was Crosbie Lucifer?

Chapter 19

The night before the lorry was going to take them into Baghdad, Richard found Victoria alone in the living room, sitting with a book.

'What are you reading?'

'You don't have much fiction here. It's *A Tale of Two Cities*. I always thought Dickens would be boring. But I'm finding it most exciting.'

'Where have you got to?' He looked over her shoulder and read out, 'And the <u>knitting</u> women count one.'

'I think she's very frightening,' said Victoria.

'Madame Defarge? Yes. Though I have always doubted that you could work a list of names into your knitting. But then I can't knit.'

'Oh I think you could,' said Victoria, considering how she would manage it by making lots of deliberate mistakes with the stitches. 'Yes, it could be done . . . '

Suddenly two things came together in her mind with the force of an explosion. The man with the hand-knitted red scarf – and that name, Lefarge.

Not Lefarge. Carmichael had not said Lefarge. It was Defarge! And of course he meant Madame Defarge.

She was brought back to reality by Richard saying, 'Is anything wrong?'

'No – no, that is, I just thought of something.'

'I see.' Richard raised his eyebrows in his most superior way. 'Your last name perhaps?'

'I know my own name,' Victoria said annoyed.

'That's not quite true,' said Richard smiling. 'It's no good, Victoria. You've been very clever. You've studied your subject and you know something about it – but I've laid traps for you. I've said some completely ridiculous things about archaeology and you've accepted them.' He paused. 'You're not Venetia Savile. Who are you?'

'I told you the first time I met you,' said Victoria. 'I'm Victoria Jones.'

'Dr Pauncefoot Jones' niece?'

'No – but my name is Jones.'

'You told me a lot of other things.'

'Yes, I did. And they were all true! But you didn't believe me. And that made me mad, because though I do tell lies   what I told you then wasn't a lie. And so I said my name was Pauncefoot Jones – I've said that before out here, and it's always worked very well. How could I have known you were actually coming to this place?'

'It must have been a shock,' said Richard seriously. 'But you did very well.'

'Inside I was absolutely terrified,' said Victoria. 'But I felt that if I waited until I got here to explain, at least I would be safe.'

'Safe? Look here, Victoria, was that wild story you told me about being chloroformed really true?'

'Of course it was true! If I wanted to invent a story, I could make up a much better one than that, and tell it better!'

'Knowing you as I do now, I can see that!'

'So why are you willing to think it's possible now?'

Richard said slowly, 'Because if, as you say, you were mixed up in Carmichael's death – well, then it might be true.'

'That's how it all began,' said Victoria.

She told him of the night of Carmichael's death, of her talk with Mr Dakin, of her journey to Basrah, of her job in the Olive Branch, of Catherine's dislike of Dr Rathbone and the very strange business of the dyed hair. The only things she left out were the red scarf and Madame Defarge.

Richard sat back and looked at her. 'Is this real? Are you real? And are you the heroine in danger, or the evil adventurer?'

Victoria said in a practical manner, 'The real point is, what are we going to say to Dr Pauncefoot Jones about me?'

'Nothing,' said Richard.

Chapter 20

Victoria, Richard and Dr Pauncefoot Jones started for Baghdad early. It took nearly three uncomfortable hours in the bumping lorry before it left them at the Tio Hotel. A lot of mail was waiting for Dr Pauncefoot Jones and Richard.

Marcus appeared, smiling his usual friendly welcome for Victoria. 'You do not come to my hotel for two weeks. Why is that? You lunch here today?'

Clearly, the kidnapping of Victoria had not been noticed. Possibly Edward had not been to the police.

'Is Mr Dakin in Baghdad, do you know, Marcus?' she asked.

'Mr Dakin – ah yes, very nice man – of course, he is a friend of yours. He was here yesterday.'

'Do you know where his office is?'

'Sure I know. Everybody knows the Iraqi Iranian Oil Company.'

'Well, I want to go there now. In a taxi.'

Marcus immediately shouted at a servant to get a taxi. Then Marcus took Victoria out and instructed the driver.

'And can I have a room?' Victoria asked.

'Yes, yes. I can give you a beautiful room and I order you a big steak – very special. And before that we can have a little drink.'

'Lovely,' said Victoria. 'Oh Marcus, can you lend me some money?'

'Of course, my dear. Here you are.'

The taxi started off suddenly with a noisy honk of its horn and Victoria fell back on the seat holding coins and notes.

Five minutes later Victoria entered the offices of the Iraqi Iranian Oil Company.

Mr Dakin rose from his desk and shook her hand as she was shown in.

'Miss – er – Miss Jones, isn't it? Bring coffee, Abdullah.'

As the door closed behind the clerk, Victoria said quietly, 'There's something I've got to tell you at once – before anything more happens to me.'

'Happens to you? Has anything happened to you?'

'Don't you know?' asked Victoria. 'Hasn't Edward told you?'

'No.'

'That jealous Catherine!'

'Pardon!'

'I bet she told Edward some silly story and the idiot believed her.'

'Well, let's hear about it,' said Mr Dakin. 'Er – if I may say so,' his eye went to Victoria's blonde head, 'I prefer you as a brunette.'

'That's only part of it,' said Victoria.

There was a knock at the door and Abdullah entered with little cups of sweet coffee.

When he had gone, Victoria began the story of her adventures. She finished by telling him about the red scarf Carmichael had dropped and how she connected it with Madame Defarge – and the idea that a message was knitted into the scarf.

'I think,' said Dakin, his eyes shining with excitement, 'that this is the first real success we've had. Where is the scarf?'

'With the rest of my things – when I packed, I put everything in.'

'And you never mentioned to anyone that that scarf belonged to Carmichael?'

'No, I'd forgotten about it.'

'Then it ought to be all right. Even if they've searched your things, they won't have seen any importance in an old scarf. All we've got to do is have your things collected. '

'I've booked a room at the Tio – but do you want me to go back to the Olive Branch?'

Dakin looked at her with interest. 'Are you scared?'

Victoria lifted her head. She had to earn her pay and show a brave face! 'I'll go if you like,' she said with a determination she did not feel.

'No. Someone learned why you were there. You'd better stay away.' He smiled. 'Otherwise you may be a redhead next time I see you.'

'That's what I want to know most of all,' cried Victoria. 'Why did they dye my hair? I can't see any reason. Can you?'

'Only so your dead body might be less easy to identify.'

'But if they wanted me dead, why didn't they kill me immediately?'

'That's the question I wish we could answer most of all, Victoria. And I haven't got a clue.'

'Talking of clues,' said Victoria, 'do you remember my saying that there was something about Sir Rupert Crofton Lee that didn't seem right, that morning at the Tio?'

'Yes.'

'You didn't know him personally, did you?'

'No.'

'I thought not. Because, you see, the man you met wasn't Sir Rupert Crofton Lee.'

And she began another story, starting with the boil on Sir Rupert's neck.

'So that was how it was done,' said Dakin. 'Carmichael got safely to Crofton Lee, but it was the Crofton Lee impersonator who stabbed him. Victoria, I want you to write to Edward now. Say you're at the Tio and ask him to bring your luggage. I'm going to see Dr Rathbone this morning about one of his meetings. It will be easy for me to quietly pass a note to his secretary personally – so there will be no danger of your enemy Catherine 'losing' it.'

Chapter 21

Victoria sat on the balcony of the Tio Hotel, once more in the role of a modern Juliet, waiting for Romeo. And soon enough Romeo appeared below, looking around.

'Edward,' Victoria called.

Edward looked up. 'Oh, there you are!'

A moment later he came out upon the balcony – and stared at her in a puzzled way. 'I say, Victoria, haven't you done something to your hair?'

Victoria gave a troubled sigh.

'I liked it better as it was,' said Edward.

'Tell Catherine so!'

'Catherine? What has she got to do with it?'

'Everything,' said Victoria. 'You told me to make friends with her, and I did, and I don't suppose you've any idea what trouble it got me into!'

'Well, Catherine said you'd told her to tell me that you'd gone off to Mosul. It was very important and good news, and I would hear from you as soon as you could manage.'

'And you believed that?' said Victoria. How could he be so silly? 'You didn't think that Catherine might be lying, and that I'd been knocked on the head.'

'What?' Edward stared.

'Chloroformed.'

'Good Lord!' Edward looked quickly around. 'I don't think we should talk out here. Can't we go to your room?'

'All right. Did you bring my luggage?'

'Yes, I left it with the porter.'

'Because I haven't had a change of clothes for two weeks . . .'

'Victoria, what has been happening? I know – I've got the car here. Let's go out to Devonshire.'

'Devonshire?' Victoria stared in surprise.

'Oh, it's just a name for a place not far out of Baghdad. It's lovely this time of year. Come on. I haven't been alone with you for so long.'

They ran down the stairs and out to where Edward's car was parked. Edward drove south along a wide road. Then he turned off and they bumped through the fields of palm trees and over little bridges. Finally they came to some fruit trees which were just beginning to flower. It was beautiful – and beyond the woods was the Tigris.

They got out and walked through the flowering trees.

'This is lovely,' said Victoria sighing deeply.

The air was soft and warm. After a while they sat down on a fallen tree with pink flowers above their heads.

'Now, darling,' said Edward. 'Tell me what's been happening to you. I've been so horribly miserable.'

'Have you?' she smiled dreamily.

Then she told him. Of the hairdresser, the chloroform – and waking up. Of how she had escaped and her lucky meeting with Richard Baker, and pretending to be an anthropologist arriving from England.

At this point Edward shouted with laughter.

'You are marvellous, Victoria! The things you think of – and invent.'

'I know,' said Victoria. 'My uncles: Dr Pauncefoot Jones and before him – the Bishop.'

And she suddenly remembered what she had been going to ask Edward at Basrah when Mrs Clayton had called them in for drinks.

'I meant to ask you before,' she said. 'How did you know about the Bishop?'

She felt his hand go tense. He said quickly, 'Why, you told me, didn't you?'

It was strange, Victoria thought afterwards, that one silly mistake should have done what it did. For he was taken by surprise, he had no story ready – his face was suddenly unguarded and his hidden lies were so easy to read.

As she looked at him, everything changed and she saw the truth. Perhaps it was not really sudden. Perhaps, pushed deep down in her mind beneath all the excitement and glamour, the question had been worrying her – How did Edward know about the Bishop?

And she had been slowly arriving at the only answer – Edward had not learned about the Bishop of Llangow from her. And the only other person he could have learned it from was Mr or Mrs Hamilton Clipp. But they had not seen Edward since her arrival in Baghdad because Edward had been in Basrah, so he must have learned it from them before he left England. He must have known all the time that Victoria was coming out to Baghdad with them – and the whole wonderful coincidence was not, after all, a coincidence.

It had been planned.

And as she stared at Edward's face, she knew, suddenly, what Carmichael had meant by Lucifer. She knew what he had seen that day as he looked along the passage to the Consulate garden. He had seen that young, beautiful face that she was looking at now – for it was beautiful, just like Lucifer, Son of the Morning, was also beautiful.

Not Dr Rathbone – it had been Edward! Edward, playing the part of the secretary, but controlling and planning and directing everything, using Rathbone as a cover-up.

As she looked at that beautiful evil face, all her silly, childish love slowly disappeared, and she knew that what she felt for Edward had never been love. It had been attraction and excitement. And Edward had never loved her. He had used his charm deliberately. He had chatted to her that day, using his charm so easily, so naturally, that she had believed him immediately. She had been a fool.

It was extraordinary how much could flash through your mind in just a few seconds. You didn't have to think about it. It just came. Full and immediate knowledge. Perhaps because really, underneath, you had known it all along . . .

Suddenly Victoria knew, instinctively, that she was in great danger. There was only one thing that could save her, only one thing she could say. 'You knew all the time that I was coming out here! You must have arranged it. Oh Edward, you are wonderful!'

Her face showed one emotion – <u>adoration</u>. And she saw the <u>scorn</u>, the relief. She could almost feel Edward saying to himself, 'The little fool! She'll believe anything! I can do what I like with her.'

'But how did you arrange it?' she said. 'You must be very powerful. You must be quite different from what you pretend to be. You're – you're like a King of Babylon.'

She saw the pride in his face. She saw the power and strength and beauty and cruelty that had been hidden behind his mask of a modest, likeable young man.

She said quickly and anxiously, as a final artistic touch, 'But you do love me, don't you?'

His scorn was clear to see now. This little fool – all women were fools! It was so easy to make them think you loved them and that was all they cared about! They had no idea of greatness, of a new world, they just wanted love! They were <u>slaves</u> and you used them as slaves.

'Of course I love you,' he said.

'But what is it all about, Edward?'

'It's a new world, Victoria. A new world that we can create from the ruins of the old.'

'Tell me.'

He told her the dream: how the old powers must destroy each other. How the fat capitalists holding on to all their money and the stupid communists who hated all ideas but their own, must destroy each other. There must be total war between America and Russia – total destruction of both. And then the new <u>Heaven</u> and the new Earth would appear. The small chosen group of superior beings – the scientists, the agricultural experts, the administrators – the young men like Edward – the young men of the New World. All young, all believing in their rule as Supermen. When the destruction was complete, they would step in and take control.

It was madness.

'But think,' said Victoria, 'of all the people who will be killed.'

'That doesn't matter,' said Edward.

But surely, Victoria thought, all the ordinary people working quietly, bringing up families and laughing and crying, they were the people who did matter. Not these angels with evil faces who didn't care who they hurt.

And carefully, for she knew that death might be very near, Victoria said, 'You are wonderful, Edward. But what can I do?'

'You want to help? You believe in it?'

She had to be careful. A sudden change would be too much.

'I think I just believe in you!' she said. 'Anything you tell me to do, Edward, I'll do.'

'Good girl.'

'Why did you arrange for me to come out here? There must have been a reason.'

'Of course. Do you remember I took a photo of you that day?'

'I remember,' said Victoria.

'I couldn't believe how much you look like a woman who's been causing us a lot of trouble. I took that photo to make sure.'

'Who is it?'

'Anna Scheele.'

Victoria stared at him in surprise. Whatever she had expected, it was not this.

'You mean Anna Scheele looks like me?'

'Quite remarkably so – and you're alike in height and size, though she's five years older than you. The real difference is the hair, you're a brunette and she's a blonde. Your eyes are a darker blue, but that wouldn't matter with sunglasses.'

'And that's why you wanted me to come to Baghdad? Because I looked like her.'

'Yes.'

'So you arranged the whole thing. The Clipps – who are the Clipps?'

'They're not important – they just do as they're told.'

Something in Edward's voice made Victoria shudder. Edward, she thought, believes he is God. That's what's so frightening.

'Anna Scheele is incredibly good with finances,' Edward was saying. 'She's found out about our financial operations. She knows how we are moving our money and what we are using it for. Three people have been dangerous to us – Rupert Crofton Lee and Carmichael – well, they're both dead. Anna Scheele is the only one left. She said she would be in Baghdad for the Conference in three days' time. But she's disappeared.'

'Disappeared? Where?'

'We've an idea,' said Edward. 'We've got someone watching every entry into this country. We know she won't use her own name – but there is a passage booked by BOAC in the name of Grete Harden. We've checked on Grete Harden – and there's no such person. The name and the address are fake. We think that Grete Harden is Anna Scheele.'

He added, 'Her plane will land at Damascus the day after tomorrow.'

'And then?'

Edward's eyes looked suddenly into hers. 'You'll take her place, Victoria.'

Like Rupert Crofton Lee, Victoria thought – and he had died. And when Victoria took her place, Anna Scheele would die.

And if for one moment Edward doubted her <u>loyalty</u>, then Victoria would die.

She must agree – and then find a way to report to Mr Dakin.

She took a deep breath, 'Oh, Edward, I'd be discovered. My voice won't sound the same as hers.'

'Anna Scheele will be suffering from a serious throat infection. Our doctor will say so.'

'Then what would I have to do?' Victoria asked.

'Fly from Damascus to Baghdad as Grete Harden. Go to bed immediately. Then the doctor will give you permission to get up just in time to go to the Conference. There, before the world's leaders, you will present *our* papers in place of Anna Scheele's.'

'What will the documents say?'

Edward smiled. 'Details that prove the most terrifying and huge communist <u>plot</u> in America.'

Victoria thought: how well they've planned it.

Victoria asked, 'What about Dr Rathbone?'

Edward smiled in cruel amusement. 'Rathbone has been stealing most of the money which comes to him from all over the world. He's dishonest – and completely in our control. All things work towards our New Order.'

Victoria thought to herself, 'Edward is mad! You get mad, perhaps, if you try and act the part of God. Humility is what keeps you human . . .'

Edward got up. 'Time to go. We've got to get you to Damascus.'

* * *

In the suburbs of Baghdad, Edward drove into a side street of modern, European-style villas with balconies and gardens round them. In front of one house a big car was standing. Edward stopped behind it.

A thin, dark-skinned woman came out to meet them and Edward spoke to her in French – it seemed that Victoria's clothes must be changed at once.

The woman turned to her and said politely in French, 'Come with me, please.'

She led Victoria into a bedroom where, lying on a bed, were the long, black clothes of a <u>nun</u>. The woman made a sign, and Victoria undressed and put them on. The French woman put a string of wooden beads over her head. Then Victoria was sent out to Edward.

'You look all right,' he said in approval. 'Keep your eyes down when there are men about.'

The Frenchwoman joined them, dressed in the same way. The two nuns got into the car which now had a tall European in the driver's seat.

'Do exactly as you are told now, Victoria,' said Edward.

There was danger behind the words.

'Aren't you coming, Edward?' Victoria begged.

He smiled at her. 'You'll see me in three days.' Then, in his charming way, he said quietly, 'Don't fail me, darling. Only you can do this – I love you, Victoria. It's too dangerous to kiss a nun – but I'd like to.'

Victoria dropped her eyes like a good nun should, but actually it was to hide her anger.

'Horrible traitor,' she thought.

'Don't worry,' Edward added. 'Your new name is Sister Marie. Sister Therese here has all the papers for the Syrian border.'

He stepped back, waved cheerfully, and the car started off.

Victoria had noticed that 'Sister Therese' had hidden a small gun in her sleeve. But there would be a moment Victoria could no longer be controlled – when she was standing with her fake documents in front of the Conference – and Edward would not be there.

No one could stop her then from saying, 'I am not Anna Scheele and these papers are untrue.'

She wondered why Edward did not fear her doing just that.

* * *

The big aeroplane made a perfect landing. The passengers going on from London to Basrah were separated from those who were catching a connecting plane to Baghdad.

There were four of these: a rich-looking Iraqi businessman, a young English doctor and two women. A dark-skinned woman with a tired face answered the airport officer's questions first.

'Mrs Pauncefoot Jones? British. Yes. To join your husband in Baghdad, please? What money have you?'

A thin, fair-haired young woman wearing dark glasses took her turn next.

'Grete Harden. Yes. Nationality? Danish. From London. Purpose of visit? Nurse at hospital. What money have you?'

The passengers were told that the Baghdad plane would leave that afternoon. They would be driven now to a hotel for a rest and lunch.

Grete Harden was sitting on her bed when a knock came on the door. She opened it and found a tall, dark-haired young woman wearing a BOAC uniform.

'I'm so sorry, Miss Harden. Would you come with me to the BOAC office? There is a difficulty with your ticket. This way, please.'

Grete Harden followed her guide down the passage. On a door was a large board lettered in gold – BOAC office.

The air hostess opened the door and directed her inside. As Grete Harden went through, she closed the door and quickly took down the board.

As soon as Grete Harden entered the room, two men put a cloth over her head, forced a ball of cloth into her mouth, and one of them, a doctor, gave her an injection.

Her body relaxed immediately.

The doctor said cheerfully, 'That will keep her unconscious for about six hours. Now then, you two, hurry up.'

He nodded towards two other people in the room. They were nuns. The men went out and the elder of the two nuns went to Grete Harden and began to take the clothes off her still body. The younger nun, shaking a little, started to undress. Soon she was wearing Grete Harden's clothes.

The two men came in again, and now they were smiling.

'Grete Harden looks just like Anna Scheele,' one said. 'And she had the papers in her luggage to prove it. Now then, Miss Harden,' he bowed to Victoria, laughing at her, 'come with me.'

The Baghdad plane left at three o'clock. The flight was short and for the second time, Victoria saw the city below her, the Tigris dividing it in a line of gold.

In two days the two great powers of the world, Russia and America, would meet to discuss the future.

And she would have a part to play.

Chapter 22

'You know,' said Richard Baker, 'I'm worried about that girl.'

Dr Pauncefoot Jones said, 'What girl?'

'Victoria.'

'Victoria?' Dr Pauncefoot Jones looked about. 'My goodness, we came back without her yesterday, didn't we?'

'I wondered if you had noticed,' said Richard.

'Very wrong of me. Didn't she know where to find the lorry?'

'She wasn't planning to come back here,' said Richard frowning. 'But she went off in a car with a young man, it seems, and she didn't come back. What's more, she hadn't opened her luggage. That seems very strange to me. And we had agreed to meet for lunch. I hope nothing's happened to her.'

'Oh, I'm sure she's fine,' said Dr Pauncefoot Jones comfortably.

'They've kidnapped her once,' said Richard. 'What's to prevent them kidnapping her again? Would you mind, sir, if I went into Baghdad again tomorrow? I'm worried about that girl. I really am.'

Dr Pauncefoot Jones suddenly gave his colleague his full attention. 'Dear me, Richard, I had no idea that you had *that* kind of interest in her. Of course, Victoria is most attractive. You've got good taste, Richard, I will admit that.'

'There's nothing of that kind,' said Richard, going red and looking even more superior than usual. 'I'm just – er – worried about her. I must go back to Baghdad.'

★ ★ ★

'You!' said Victoria with dislike.

Taken up to her room in the Babylonian Palace Hotel in Baghdad, the first person she saw was Catherine dressed as a nurse.

Catherine nodded with equal hatred.

'Yes. It is I, you stupid English girl. Edward has never cared for you,' she continued full of scorn. 'It is me Edward loves!'

Looking at her hard, <u>fanatical</u> face, Victoria said, 'Anybody could do your hospital nurse act. The whole thing depends on me doing mine. I'm <u>indispensable</u>.'

Catherine whispered with hatred, 'Nobody is indispensable.'

★ ★ ★

The telephone rang and was quickly answered.

'American Embassy. How can I help?'

'This is Dr Smallbrook,' the caller repeated, as soon as a suitably important Embassy official had been called to the phone. 'I am looking after Miss Scheele who has a serious throat infection. Miss Scheele has some important papers with her and would like some responsible person from the Embassy to come to the Babylonian Palace Hotel and collect them. Immediately. Thank you. I will be waiting for you.'

★ ★ ★

Victoria turned from the mirror. She was wearing an expensive, well-made suit. Every blonde hair was carefully styled. She felt nervous but excited.

As she turned, she caught a nasty look in Catherine's eyes and was suddenly on her guard.

'What are you so pleased about?'

'Soon you will see.' Catherine's hatred was ugly. 'You think you are so clever. You think everything depends on you. Pah! You are a fool.'

A knock came on the door.

'Now you will see!' cried Catherine.

The door opened and a man came in. He was dressed in the uniform of the International Police. He locked the door behind him. Then he turned towards Victoria. As he looked at her, she saw that the heavy wooden stick carried by the police was already in his hand. She knew then what Catherine meant – what the real plan was. They had never intended her to play the part of Anna Scheele at the Conference. How could they risk that? No, the plan had always been that Anna Scheele would be killed at the last moment – killed in such a way that her face would not be recognizable. Only the fake papers would remain.

Victoria screamed. And with a smile, the man came towards her.

There was the crash of a breaking window – a heavy hand sent Victoria down on to the floor – she saw stars – and blackness. Then out of the blackness a wonderful English voice said, 'Are you all right, Miss?'

★ ★ ★

The telephone rang and Dakin picked it up.

An English voice said, 'Operation Victoria was successful.'

'Good,' said Dakin.

'We've got Catherine and the doctor. The other man was fatally injured.'

'No news still of the real Anna Scheele?'

'No news at all.'

Dakin put down the phone.

He was very glad to hear that Victoria was all right. But Anna herself, Dakin thought, must be dead. She had refused all help, had gone her own way – though she had repeated that she would be in Baghdad without fail on the 19th. Today was the 19th and there was no Anna Scheele. Perhaps she had been right not to trust the official organization – but apparently her own intelligence had been no better.

And without Anna Scheele, the evidence was not complete.

A messenger came in with a note: Mr Richard Baker and Mrs Pauncefoot Jones are here to see you about Carmichael.

'Show them in,' said Dakin.

Richard Baker and Mrs Pauncefoot Jones came in. Baker said, 'I was at school with a man I knew as Henry "Fakir" Carmichael. When I was at Basrah a few weeks ago, I met him in the Consulate waiting room, dressed as an Arab. Does this interest you?'

'Very much,' said Dakin.

'Carmichael was attacked and ran away but before he went, he slipped something into my pocket. The other day I learnt from Victoria Jones that he was dead – and you were the right person to deliver this to.'

He placed the dirty chit on Dakin's desk.

Dakin sighed deeply.

'This means more than you can possibly imagine.' He got up. 'I'm very grateful to you, Baker. Forgive me, but there is a lot I have to do without wasting a minute.'

He shook hands with Mrs Pauncefoot Jones saying, 'I suppose you are joining your husband at the dig. I hope you have a good season.'

'It's a good thing Pauncefoot Jones didn't come into Baghdad with me,' said Richard. 'He would probably have noticed the difference between his wife and his wife's sister.'

Mrs Pauncefoot Jones said in a low, pleasant voice, 'My sister Elsie is still in England. I dyed my hair black and came out on her passport. My sister's name before she married was Elsie Scheele. My name, Mr Dakin, is Anna Scheele.'

Chapter 23

Baghdad had been transformed. American and Russian Police lined the streets as the news went round. The President of the United States and the Russian leader were in Baghdad. They were in the Regent's Palace.

At last the great Conference had begun.

'What makes me sad,' said Victoria, sitting on the terrace overlooking the river at the Tio Hotel, 'is that poor woman who got killed in my place in Damascus.'

'Oh! She's all right,' said Mr Dakin cheerfully. 'As soon as your plane had taken off, we arrested the French woman and took Grete Harden to hospital. She was one of our people of course.'

'Was she?'

'Yes, when Anna Scheele disappeared, we thought it might be a good idea to give the other side something to think about. So we booked a ticket for Grete Harden – and gave her false papers showing she was Anna Scheele.'

'And the real Anna Scheele came out as Mrs Pauncefoot Jones.'

'Yes. Anna is a very clever young woman.'

'I really thought I was going to die,' said Victoria. 'But your people were watching over me.'

'All the time. Your Edward wasn't quite so clever as he thought. Actually we had been watching Edward Goring for some time. When you told me your story, the night Carmichael was killed, I was very worried about you. The best thing I could think of was to send you in as a spy. If your Edward knew that you were in touch with me, you'd be reasonably safe. You'd be too valuable to kill because he'd be using you to find out what we were doing. And he could also pass on false information to us through you. But then you told him you knew about the false Rupert Crofton Lee, and Edward decided it would be better to keep you safely out of the way until you were needed for the impersonation of Anna Scheele. Yes, Victoria, you're very lucky to be sitting where you are now.'

'I know I am.' Victoria looked at him steadily. 'Next time I fall in love, it won't be for excitement and good looks. I'd like a real man – not one who says pretty things to me. I don't mind if he's bald or wears glasses. I'd like him to be interesting – and know about interesting things.'

'About thirty-five or fifty-five?' asked Mr Dakin.

Victoria looked surprised. 'Oh, thirty-five.'

'I am so happy. I thought for a moment you were offering to marry me.'

Victoria laughed. 'And was there a message knitted into the scarf?'

'There was a name. The scarf and the chit were the two halves of the clue. The scarf gave us the name of Sheikh Hussein el Ziyara of Kerbela. He and Carmichael had been friends since they were children. The chit, when treated with chemicals, gave us the code words to persuade the Sheikh to give us Carmichael's proof – a packet of microfilms.'

'And it was carried through the country by those two wandering cinema men – the ones we actually met?'

'Yes. They met him when he came down from the mountains. He spent four days crossing the desert in their company. Simple, well-known men. Nothing political about them. Just Carmichael's friends. He had a lot of friends.'

'He must have been very nice. I'm sorry he's dead.'

'If there's another life after this, and I fully believe that there is,' said Mr Dakin, 'he'll have the satisfaction of knowing that his courage has saved this sad old world from a fresh attack of war and misery. All the evidence that he and Sir Rupert and Anna Scheele collected is now before the President of America and the Premier of the USSR.'

'It's strange, isn't it,' said Victoria thoughtfully, 'that Richard had one half of the secret and I had the other. It almost seems as though . . .'

'As though it were meant to be,' finished Mr Dakin with a twinkle in his eye. 'And what are you going to do next, may I ask?'

'I will have to find a job,' said Victoria. 'I must start looking.'

'Don't look too hard,' said Mr Dakin. 'I think a job is coming towards you.'

He walked away to make room for Richard Baker.

'Look here, Victoria,' said Richard. 'Venetia Savile can't come out to the dig after all. Apparently she's ill. You were quite useful out there. Would you like to come back? We can only offer to pay for your food, I'm afraid. And probably your passage back to England – but we'll talk about that later. Well, what do you say?'

'Oh, do you really want me?' cried Victoria.

For some reason Richard Baker went very pink in the face. 'I think,' he said, 'we could find you – er – very useful.'

'I'd love that,' replied Victoria.

CHARACTER LIST

Captain Crosbie: an Englishman living in Baghdad

Mr Dakin: an Englishman living in Baghdad who works with Captain Crosbie

Henry (Fakir) Carmichael: a British Intelligence agent

Salah Hassan: owner of a shop in Basrah

Sir Rupert Crofton Lee: a famous traveller

Anna Scheele: a secretary at the Morganthal International Bank in America

Otto Morganthal: head of the Bank

Victoria Jones: a young English girl who is looking for adventure

Edward Goring: a very handsome young Englishman, secretary to Dr Rathbone

Dr Rathbone: an Englishman living in Baghdad, founder of The Olive Branch, a charitable book business in Baghdad

Sanders: an agent watching Anna Scheele

Mrs Hamilton Clipp: an American lady travelling to Baghdad

Mr George Hamilton Clipp: her husband

Dr Pauncefoot Jones: a famous English archaeologist working at a site near Baghdad

Richard Baker: an English archaeologist who works for Dr Pauncefoot Jones

Gerald Clayton: the British Consul-General in Basrah

Archie Gaunt: the British Consul in Kuwait

Rosa Clayton: married to Gerald Clayton

Robert Hall: an English businessman

Marcus Tio: owner of the Tio Hotel in Baghdad

Mrs Cardew Trench: an Englishwoman staying at the Tio Hotel

Catherine: a volunteer who works at The Olive Branch

Ibrahim: a servant at the archaeological dig

Venetia Savile: an English anthropologist

Abdullah: a clerk at the Iraqi Iranian Oil Company

Grete Harden: a passenger on a flight to Damascus

Sister Therese: a French woman working for Edward

Dr Smallbrook: a doctor in Baghdad

Mrs Elsie Pauncefoot Jones: wife of the archaeologist

CULTURAL NOTES

Map of Iraq and the region in 1951

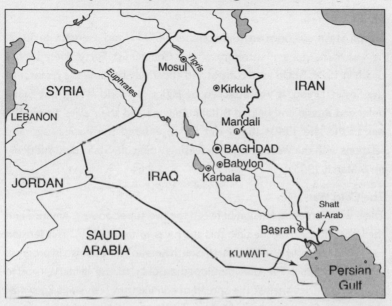

Iraq

For centuries the countries we know today as Iraq and Iran had been ruled by the Turks as part of the Ottoman Empire. After the defeat of the empire at the end of the First World War (1918), Britain and France took control of large areas of land and formed two new states – Iran and Iraq. At the time the story was written (1951) Britain had a strong interest in the region, especially because of its oil.

The High Command

The High Command is the group of most senior military officers in a nation's armed forces.

Stalin

Joseph Stalin was born on 18 December 1879 in Gori, Georgia. In 1922, he was made general secretary of the Communist Party. After Lenin's death in 1924, Stalin took control and effectively became the dictator of the Soviet Union. It was attacked by Hitler in World War II but Stalin defended Russia and helped Britain, America and their allies to win the war. In the late 1940s the Soviet Union entered the nuclear age and relations with the West became increasingly difficult. Stalin died suddenly on 5 March 1953.

The Cold War

There was increasing tension between the two super powers, America and the USSR (Russia), at the time this story was written (1951). This tension was called the Cold War. The North-South Korean War was also in progress at the same time. The USA developed a policy to use military force to protect countries against the spread of communism – this was known as the Truman Doctrine. A conference like the one imagined in the story between the US President and the Russian leader would have been very important as a measure to reduce tension and promote better relations.

Idealism

Idealism was typical in the post-war years. In the story, there are references to some extreme idealists who believed it was necessary to destroy the known political and social systems in order to start a 'new world'. This added threat of violence complicated the already existing situation of tension between the two super powers. This idealism attracted young people with modern ideas, perhaps symbolized in a light-hearted way in the story by the amusing reference to women wearing trousers in The Olive Branch – something unusual for the time.

Romeo and Juliet

These are the famous lovers in Shakespeare's play. It is an impossible love because they come from two families who are enemies.

Ritz and Savoy Hotels

These were and still are two of the best, and most well-known, luxury hotels in London. Victoria deliberately chose to use notepaper from these hotels to impress anyone who read her references.

A bishop in the Church of England

A bishop in the Church of England is a very senior priest who is responsible for an area in the UK or overseas. Some bishops sit in the House of Lords in the British parliament and have great authority. By writing a false letter from a bishop, Victoria is trying to impress her employer.

Llangow

Llangow is the name of a fictional place in Wales – the double 'l' is typical of place names in Wales and has a particular pronunciation – something like 'hla'.

Morse code

This is the international system of representing letters and numbers, each with a unique number of dots (short signal) and dashes (long signal). It was used for radio communication before voice transmission was possible. The most well-known Morse code message means 'emergency' – SOS. This message consists of 3 short dots for 'S' and 3 long dashes for 'O'. So, SOS is represented by 'dot-dot-dot-dash-dash-dash-dot-dot-dot'.

Eton

Eton is a famous independent school in Britain. It is very expensive. Over the last six centuries, it has produced many of Britain's Prime Ministers, leading politicians, embassy and top army personnel and judges. Most British princes have also been educated there. Usually boys board (live) there and life-long friendships and business associations are a typical result. Richard Baker and Carmichael would have a close friendship because of this.

A dig
Agatha Christie was married to a well-known archaeologist and accompanied him on many 'digs'. A dig is where a section of ground is excavated by archaeologists in a very careful and methodical way, to find ancient remains of buildings, tools, pottery, and other signs showing how ancient civilizations lived.

BOAC
This abbreviation stands for British Overseas Airways Corporation. BOAC and BEA (British European Airways) joined together in 1974 to become British Airways – now Britain's most famous air company.

The Olive Branch
An olive branch is a symbol of peace. In the story the organization is run by idealists who say they want to work for world peace, unity and brotherhood.

Lucifer
The name Lucifer – which means 'carrying or bringing light' – became associated in religious contexts with the Devil or Satan. Lucifer is described as being very beautiful. In the story, Lucifer must be someone who appears to be good, and perhaps handsome too, when in fact he is bad.

Lefarge/Defarge
A Tale of Two Cities is one of Charles Dickens' most famous novels. It is set during the time of the French Revolution in France (in the 1770s). The reference in our story to Madame Defarge (a character in Dickens' story) is connected with the fact that she puts the names of people to be killed into a special code in her knitting, by changing the type and appearance of the stitches used.

Babylon

Babylon was an ancient city in Mesopotamia, which was built during the period of Nebuchadnezzar II (604–562 BC). It became famous for its 'Hanging Gardens' which were known as one of the Seven Wonders of the World.

In the story Victoria and Edward visit the ruins of the ancient city of Babylon, situated about 85 kilometres south of Baghdad.

A tell

A tell is a hill which is the result of the building and rebuilding of mud-brick towns over the centuries. As the old buildings fell down, the ground was flattened and new buildings were built on top of the old. In this way, over time, the height of the hill grew. They are of great interest to archaeologists and anthropologists.

The Great Exhibition

The Great Exhibition was held in London in 1851 to show to the world Great Britain's industrial, economic and military power. Countries from all over the civilized world were invited to attend and display their inventions. Over six million visitors viewed the 13,000 items displayed in the specially constructed Crystal Palace in Hyde Park.

Kerbela or Karbala

Kerbela is one of the holy cities for Shi'a Muslims. This city contains many holy places and is visited by hundreds of thousands of pilgrims each year.

Glossary

adoration (n)

loving and admiring someone

alley (n)

a narrow passage or street with buildings or walls on both sides

ambulance (n)

a vehicle for taking people to and from hospital

angel (n)

a spiritual being that some people believe is God's messenger and servant in **Heaven**

anthropologist (n)

a person who studies humans: their origins, physical characteristics, institutions, religious **beliefs**, etc.

archaeologist (n)

a person who studies the past by examining the remains of things such as buildings and tools

as a matter of fact (exp)

used to emphasize the importance and truth of the following information

attentive (adj)
watching or listening carefully

barber (n)
a man whose job is cutting men's hair

bargaining (n)
ability to get something for a good price

basin (n)
a deep bowl that you use for holding liquids, or for mixing food in

bazaar (n)
an area with many small shops and stalls, especially in the Middle East

BC (Before Christ)
used in dates to show a number of years or centuries before the year in
which Jesus Christ is believed to have been born

beads (n)
small pieces of coloured glass, wood, or plastic with a hole through the
middle which are worn as jewellery or used for counting or praying

belief (n)
a feeling of certainty that something exists, is true, or is good

betray (v)
to give information to an enemy, putting your country or comrades at
risk

blow-lamp (n)
a tool with a pressurized flame used when working with metal

boil (n)
a red, painful, infected spot on your skin

booking (n)
a reservation for a hotel room or a ticket at a particular time

bounce (v)
to jump up and down repeatedly; to move around a lot

bow (v)
to bend your body towards someone to show respect or to greet them

branch (n)
the part of a tree that grows out from its trunk

brim (n)
the very top part of a cup or glass, above which a liquid will come out

brotherhood (n)
an organization whose members all have the same political aims and **beliefs**

brunette (n)
a woman with brown hair

bucket (n)
a deep round metal or plastic container with a **handle**

bullet (n)
a small piece of metal which is fired from a gun

caravan (n)
a group of people and animals that travel together, especially in deserts

charm (n)
the quality of being attractive and pleasant

cheat (v)
to treat someone dishonestly

chit (n)
a short, informal letter recommending someone for a job

chloroform (n)
a colourless liquid with a strong sweet smell, which makes you unconscious

circumstances (n)
the conditions which affect what happens in a particular situation

cloak (n)
a wide, loose coat that closes at the neck and does not have sleeves

conflict (n)
fighting between countries or groups of people

Consul-General (n)
a government official who lives in a foreign city and looks after all the people there who are from his or her own country

Consulate (n)
the official building where the **Consul** works

copper (n)
soft reddish-brown metal

courtyard (n)
a flat, open area of ground surrounded by buildings or walls

crawl (v)
to move forward on your hands and knees, or with difficulty

criminal (n)
a person who has committed a crime

Customs (n)
the official organization responsible for collecting taxes on goods coming into a country and preventing illegal goods from being brought in

damn (excl)
used to express anger or impatience

date (n)
a small, sticky, dark brown fruit with a stone inside that grows on a palm tree

delighted (adj), **delight** (n)
extremely pleased and excited about something

depend (v)
if you say that one thing depends on another, you mean that the first thing will be affected or decided by the second

determination (n)
making a firm decision to do something and not letting anything stop you

dig (n)
an excavation where **archaeologists** look for ancient remains

disapproval (n)
an expression that shows you don't like something or you think that it is wrong

dismiss (v)
when the employer orders the employee to leave his job

distress (n)
the state of needing urgent help

donkey (n)
an animal like a small horse with long ears

doubtfully (adv)
doing something in an uncertain way

dread (n)
a great fear

dust (n)
very small dry particles of earth, sand, or dirt

dust storm (n)
a strong wind carrying a large quantity of sand or **dust**

efficiency (n)
the ability to do tasks successfully, without wasting time or energy

Empress (n)
a woman who rules an Empire, or the wife of an Emperor

eyebrow (n)
the lines of hair which grow above your eyes

excess baggage (n)
more than the amount of luggage you are allowed to carry for the price you have paid

exhausted (adj)
very tired

fake (adj)
looking genuine or real when they are not

fanatical (adj)
very extreme

features (n)
your eyes, nose, mouth, and other parts of your face

fool (n)
someone who is not sensible and who has poor judgement

frown (v)
to move your **eyebrows** together because you are annoyed, worried, or thinking

grateful (adj)
pleased with someone and thankful for what they have done

greet (v)
to say something friendly such as 'hello' when you meet someone

hammering (n)
a loud noise produced by a heavy tool hitting something

hand-knitted (adj)
when something has been made by hand from wool using knitting needles

handle (n)
the part of an object such as a tool, bag, or cup that you hold in order to be able to pick up and use the object

Heaven (n)
according to certain religions, the place where good people are said to go when they die

hide-and-seek (n)
a children's game where some people hide and one person looks for them

horrified (adj)
shocked, disappointed, or disgusted

hysterical (adj)
a state of uncontrolled excitement or panic

impersonator (n)
a person who pretends to be someone else in order to **trick** people

indispensable (adj)
absolutely essential

Inshallah
a greeting in Arabic meaning 'God willing' – roughly, 'if God wishes it to be that way, then it will happen'

instinct (n)
a feeling that you have about a particular situation, rather than an opinion based on facts

intelligence (n)
information gathered by the government about their country's enemies

jealous (adj)
when someone feels angry or bitter because they think that another person is trying to take a lover, friend, or possession, away from them

kidnap (v)
to take someone away illegally and by force, and usually to hold them prisoner in order to demand something from their family, employer, or government

knitting (n)
something, such as a piece of clothing, that is being made by a process that requires wool and knitting needles

leak (n)
when secret or official information is told to the wrong people, either by accident or on purpose

level (v)
to make something flat or to destroy it

load (v)
to put a large quantity of things into something, often heavy things

loyalty (n)
staying firm in your friendship or support for someone or something

make up (phr v)
to invent

meant to be (exp)
destined by God or fate to happen

microfilm (n)
a film with a miniature photographic copy of something, usually documents or pictures

mission (n)
an important task that you are given to do, especially one that involves travelling to another country

misunderstandings (n)
when people don't understand each other correctly or don't agree

Morse code (n)
a system of transmitting messages as a series of on-off tones, lights or clicks (see Cultural notes)

mousetrap (n)
a device for catching mice

nickname (n)
an informal name for someone or something

nod (v)
to move your head up and down to show that you understand or you agree

nonsense (n)
something that you think is untrue or silly

nun (n)
a member of a female religious community

olive (n)
a type of tree which has small green or black fruits that produce good oil

on one's guard (exp)
to be very careful because you think a situation might become difficult or dangerous

on the run (exp)
running away or escaping from someone or something

owl (n)
a bird with large eyes which hunts small animals at night

parachute (v)
to jump from an aircraft using a large piece of thin cloth attached to your body by strings which enables you to float safely to the ground

password (n)
a secret word or phrase that enables you to enter a place or be recognized

persuade (v)
to get someone to do something by convincing them it is a good idea

pile (n)
a mass of things that is high in the middle and has sloping sides

pillow (n)
a rectangular cushion which you rest your head on when you are in bed

plaster (n)
a hard case used to protect broken bones

plasticine (n)
a synthetic material similar to clay used in modelling

platinum blonde (adj)
a very pale, yellow-white hair colour

plot (n)
a secret plan to do something illegal or wrong

pointless (adj)
with no purpose

pottery (n)
objects made from clay, typically plates, cups and large containers

praise (n)
an expression of approval for a person's qualities and/or achievements

preach (v)
to **persuade** other people to accept the **belief** or take the course of action

pride (n)
a feeling of satisfaction which you have because you have done, or possess, something good and important; a feeling of dignity and self-respect

proof (n)
a fact, argument, or piece of evidence which shows that something is true or exists

ragged (adj)
old and torn, used especially with clothing

railing (n)
a fence made from metal bars

recognition (n)
the act of identifying someone or something when you see it

reflection (n)
an image that you can see in a mirror or in water

relief (n)
the feeling you have when something unpleasant has not happened or is no longer happening

remain (v)
to stay in a place

robe (n)
a long, loose piece of clothing that covers what you are wearing under it

rough (adj)
with bumps and holes

scorn (n)
obvious disrespect for someone or something

sermon (n)
a talk on a religious or moral subject

Shah (n)
ruler of Persia

sheikh (n)
a male Arab chief or ruler

shimmer (v)
to shine with a faint moving or changing light

show-off (n)
someone who is trying to impress people by showing in a very obvious way what they can do or what they own

shudder (v)
to shake with disgust, horror or fear

sigh (v)
to let out a deep breath, as a way of expressing feelings such as disappointment, tiredness, or pleasure

slave (n)
a person who is owned by another person and has to work for that person without pay

sooner or later (exp)
at some point in time

souk (n)
an open-air market

sound-proof (adj)
when sound cannot penetrate

stab (v)
to push a knife into someone's body

stare (v)
to look for a long time at someone or something

steady (v)
to regain control of your body or voice

suspiciously (adv)
to act in a way which looks as if you are involved in a crime or a dishonest activity

terror (n)
a very great fear

torture (v)
to deliberately cause another person terrible pain, in order to punish them or to make them reveal information

track (n)
a narrow road or path

traitor (n)
someone who secretly helps the enemy and puts their country in danger

trick (v)
to make someone believe something is true when it isn't

twinkle (v)
to show amusement in your eyes

twist (v)
to move into an unusual, uncomfortable, or bent position

uranium (n)
a radioactive metal used to produce nuclear energy and weapons

vague (adj)
not clear, not distinct, not definite

volunteer (n)
someone who offers to do a particular task without being paid to do it

warning (n)
something that is said or written to tell people of a possible danger, problem, or other unpleasant thing that might happen

wounded (adj)
when your body is injured, especially with a cut or hole caused by a gun, knife, or similar weapon

THE AGATHA CHRISTIE SERIES

The Mysterious Affair at Styles
The Man in the Brown Suit
The Murder of Roger Ackroyd
The Murder at the Vicarage
Peril at End House
Why Didn't They Ask Evans?
Death in the Clouds
Appointment with Death
N or M?
The Moving Finger
Sparkling Cyanide
Crooked House
They Came to Baghdad
They Do It With Mirrors
A Pocket Full of Rye
After the Funeral
Destination Unknown
Hickory Dickory Dock
4.50 From Paddington
Cat Among the Pigeons

Visit **www.collinselt.com/agathachristie** for language
activities and teacher's notes based on this story.